Shalom, Geneva Peace

ALSO BY PHYLLIS SHALANT

Look What We've Brought You from Vietnam
The Rock Star, the Rooster, & Me, the Reporter
The Transformation of Faith Futterman

Shalom, Geneva Peace

By PHYLLIS SHALANT

DUTTON CHILDREN'S BOOKS

NEW YORK

LIBRARY OF CONGRESS CATALOGING-IN-PUBLICATION DATA
Shalant, Phyllis.
Shalom, Geneva Peace/by Phyllis Shalant.—1st ed.
p.   cm.
Summary: Thirteen-year-old Andi's life is changed when she befriends
the glamorous, uninhibited Geneva Peace and her Hebrew school is taken over
by a handsome rabbinic intern.
ISBN 0-525-44868-3
[1. Friendship—Fiction.   2. Jews—Fiction.]   I. Title.
PZ7.S52787Sh   1992   [Fic]—dc20   92-7348   CIP   AC

Published in the United States 1992 by
Dutton Children's Books,
a division of Penguin Books USA Inc.
375 Hudson Street, New York, New York 10014

Designed by Sylvia Frezzolini

Printed in U.S.A.
First edition
1   2   3   4   5   6   7   8   9   10

To Emily,
with thanks for sharing.

Shalom, Geneva Peace

1

*I*n the fall of eighth grade, I felt like I was trapped in the House of Mirrors at an amusement park; the kind where every mirror you pass changes you into a different person. One minute you're short and fat, the next, tall and thin; then you've got green hair and teeth, or the top of your head resembles a mushroom. Except it was my insides that were being stretched and pulled and twisted into weird shapes. Sometimes I hardly recognized myself.

I'd just begun school at the Barth Academy, which anyone who attended for an hour or so called the Barf Academy. My mother and father were convinced that their precious jewel needed a more challenging academic program than our local junior high provided, and they thought that glorious old Barf would fit the bill.

I hadn't really minded leaving the public school I'd been attending. Most of the kids in my class were jerks anyway, except for Marci, who had been my closest friend since third grade. Last spring, though, she'd begun acting sort of strange. She'd even started calling me "Brain

Trust" and "Think Tank" like some of my other class-mates. Since everyone seemed to think those nicknames were funny, I tried to laugh them off. But when they came from the lips of my best friend . . . well, it hurt.

Still, in my old school, the kids had mostly ignored me. From the first day I arrived at Barf, I seemed to stick out like a raisin in a bowl of cornflakes. For one thing, when my homeroom teacher, Ms. Taylor, introduced me as a transfer student, everyone turned and stared—which would have been normal, except they were gazing at my chest, not my face. Since my chest is flatter than Kansas, I figured they were looking at my sweatshirt. My brother, Mitchell, had sent it to me. College sweats were big in my old school, but no one else in this homeroom was wearing them.

Also, I was the only girl in the class who didn't play lacrosse. Actually, there was one other person besides me who didn't raise her hand to sign up for the girls' junior varsity tryouts that afternoon—but she had a cast on one leg. Barf was going to be challenging all right, only not quite in the way my parents expected.

When the bell rang for first period, the kids around me charged off like racehorses. Since I wasn't sure where my next class was, I stayed out of their way. Then Ms. Taylor suddenly looked up from her desk and remembered me. Like a shot, her arm reached out and grabbed the sleeve of a girl who hadn't made it out the door yet. "Alana, I believe Andi is in your math section. Would you show her where the room is, please?"

"Sure," the girl answered brightly. But as soon as Ms. Taylor's attention was back on her papers, Alana tossed her head as if she were trying to shake off a fly and pushed ahead of me out the door. "Come on," she said, "it's this way."

Two girls were waiting for her right outside the classroom. Clutching my looseleaf to my chest, I hung back slightly and waited to be introduced, but the group moved off without seeming to notice me. I trailed a few steps behind, trying to look like I wasn't following them. Together their hair formed a solid gold curtain that was nearly blinding. When they stopped and turned to face me, I practically crashed into them.

"Bonita Dickerson, Deidre Van Dorne, this is Andi Applebaum," Alana announced.

"Hi," I said, trying to sound friendly but not too friendly. Just looking at them gave me a sinking feeling. They were all tall, with the kind of healthy skin that made me vow to drink more milk.

"Does your shirt say Penn State?" the one named Deidre asked, trying to read around my notebook.

I lowered my arms slowly so she could see. "Yeah, my brother sent it to me. He's a student there." I remembered the first time I'd worn the shirt. It had been miles too big on me, but all day I'd imagined I could feel the weight of Mitchell's warm arm draped over my shoulder.

"Sweet," she cooed, smiling down at me.

I hoped she'd develop a permanent milk mustache.

"I noticed you didn't sign up for lacrosse tryouts this afternoon," Alana said. "What did you play at your old school?"

"I was cocaptain of the Knowledge Bowl team." As soon as I'd said the words, I wished I could take them back. I didn't want to sound like I was bragging, and besides, a lot of kids at my old school thought Knowledge Bowl was for weirdos.

"Knowledge Bowl?"

"It's a competition between schools to see whose team can answer more questions in math, history, science, literature, and stuff."

Alana exchanged glances with her friends. "I don't think we have that here."

"Well, we didn't have lacrosse at my old school," I told her. I was beginning to wish I was back there. Maybe the library was small and the computer lab was outdated, but at least there'd been Knowledge Bowl—and Marci.

"*Everyone* around here plays," Alana said, gazing just over my head and down the hall. "You should try it."

My mother had cautioned me to be open to new experiences. "Okay, maybe I'll—"

I was interrupted by the warning bell. Alana and her friends rushed off without waiting for me to finish.

• • •

When I got home from school, I called Marci. "So how's eighth grade at old Lazy Hollow Junior High?" I asked when she picked up the phone.

"Great! I have math and English with Sharon Merrill. We both joined the Pom Girls this afternoon."

"Oh." I tried not to act surprised. Marci and I had always laughed about the Pom Girls, whose entire job was to shake their pom-poms—which we'd referred to as dust mops—at football and basketball games. I decided to change the subject to something safer. "Who's the new cocaptain of Knowledge Bowl?"

"I don't know. I'm not playing this year. It conflicts with Pom Girls practice." She sounded edgy, like she thought I'd disapprove.

I couldn't believe she was dropping Knowledge Bowl for air dusting, but all I said was, "You have to *practice* to be a Pom Girl?"

"There are routines to learn," she said coldly.

"Yeah, I guess so." She didn't ask how my day was, so I volunteered, "I tried out for the JV lacrosse team today."

"You did?"

"Yeah. They gave me this stick with a little net at the end, which I had to hold up in front of my face. Then someone flung a hardball, which I was supposed to catch in the net before it cracked my head open."

"So did you?"

"No. I dropped the stick and jumped out of the way." We both howled hysterically at that until she got the hiccups, which she always did when she laughed really hard.

"Go drink some water. I'll hold on," I told her.

"No, don't. I mean (*hic*) I've got to get off now anyway (*hic*). Sharon and I are going shopping (*hic-hic*) for school supplies."

I felt like I'd been nailed in the chest with the lacrosse ball, but I kept my voice light and cheerful. "Tell Sharon hi for me."

"Okay. I'll call you soon."

"Yeah, sure."

2

The only part of my old life that still remained was my post–b'nai mitzvah class at Hillside Community Temple. It was a combined class made up of eighth and ninth graders who'd already had their bar or bat mitzvahs. I'd known the other eighth graders for ages, but even the ninth graders were familiar to me—including Geneva Peace.

I'd last spoken to Geneva when I was six, the year I'd started Hebrew school. She was a grade ahead of me, a wild-eyed, wild-haired kid who was well known for kicking the shins of anyone who got in her way, including me. I think my exact words to her were, "I'm telling the teacher on you," which only caused her to kick me again. After that I'd avoided her, and once past the kicking stage, she'd ignored me.

Geneva and I both chose seats at the back of the room. I couldn't help noticing how she lounged back in her chair so her legs stuck right out into the aisle. Everyone who came in after her had to step over them. I guess you could say she looked *mature*. Her body was alternately concave and convex in all the right places. Even her lips curved. She reminded me of the Mona Lisa: I couldn't tell whether she was smiling or just feeling superior to the rest of us.

And I couldn't keep my eyes off the jungle of bracelets that wound up her arm. She wore about seventeen of them—all different: Some had bright dangles that tinkled like music; others were made of woven fabric or braided leather; there were strands strung with beads of deep, earthy tones; and a few glittery bangles were decorated with bits of mirror and shiny stones. The whole collection seemed mystical, like something an ancient medicine woman would wear.

The girls at Barf each wore the same gray rope bracelet with a sailor's knot in the middle. Geneva's armful would have really given them something to whisper about.

To start things off, our teacher, Mr. Aronson, decided we should play Hebrew "Jeopardy!" He consulted his notes and chalked a lopsided game on the board. The categories were Bible, Baseball, Holidays, Israel, Language, and Literature.

"Okay, who wants to start?" he asked. He put two fingers inside his collar and ran them around the rim, waiting for a volunteer.

I forced myself to count to ten before I raised my hand. Still, it was the only hand up. "I'll take Baseball for ten dollars," I said when Mr. A. nodded at me. That got the attention of the boys in the class.

Mr. A. looked down at his list of baseball facts. "This

player shocked America when he refused to pitch a crucial game on Yom Kippur, 1961," he read. Several of the boys groaned loudly.

"Shh! None of you guys wanted to go first. You missed your chance." Mr. A. turned back to me for an answer.

In "Jeopardy!" your responses had to be phrased as questions. "Who was Sandy Koufax?" I said. The boys were right, the question was practically a giveaway. Koufax had stood up for his beliefs by publicly observing the most sacred day of his religion. He was a hero to practically every Jewish kid who'd ever cared about baseball.

Since I was right, I got to continue. "I'll take Baseball for twenty dollars."

Our teacher consulted his paper again. "This Jewish player holds the American League record for stealing home plate the most times in one season: seven steals in 1969."

"Who was Rod Carew?" I had to stifle a smile when I realized that the boys in the room had fallen absolutely silent. "I'll take Baseball for thirty dollars."

"This Jewish player hit .538 for the Mets in the 1969 championship series."

"Who was Art Shamsky?" I answered easily. Then I picked Baseball for forty dollars.

Actually, there was a good reason for my knowing so much about the game. When I was seven, my brother gave me quizzes using the tiny player biographies on the backs of his baseball cards. He had whole shoe boxes full of them, divided into categories like Current Year, World Series Winners, Rookies, All-Stars, Play-off Winners,

Play-off Losers, and Classics. And he let me dip into all of them as long as I didn't mess up his filing system.

I can still remember sitting on the shaggy brown carpet that covered the floor of his room and sounding out, "Fer-nand-oh Val-en-zoo-ela, Dodgers pitcher," while Mitchell would nod approvingly or correct my mistakes. And once a week, we'd walk to the 7-Eleven together to spend our allowance on new packs of cards. He'd trade me his stale pink gum stick for whatever he wanted from my hand and I'd never object, even though I sensed I was getting a raw deal. Finally, on my eighth birthday, he told me to pick any card I wanted from his collection, and I chose the one from Darryl Strawberry's rookie year. Boy, was he steamed.

"This player was the first Jew elected to the Baseball Hall of Fame." There was a touch of irritation in Mr. A.'s voice by now.

All my classmates were staring, even Geneva. It was the kind of reaction I sometimes got when I was on a roll at Knowledge Bowl competitions. Usually I enjoyed the attention, but now and then it made me feel uncomfortable. Although I'd never deliberately given a wrong answer, there were a few times I'd been tempted.

It wasn't my fault Mr. A. had made the game so easy, but I counted to ten, pretending to need time before I answered, "Who was Hank Greenberg?" We were down to the last question in the category. I focused my eyes on my desk, trying to look modest. "I'll take Baseball for fifty dollars."

Poor Mr. A. was sulking. "This Jewish player eventually became a part owner of the Chicago White Sox."

Surprised, I closed my mouth. The only possibility I could think of was Hank Greenberg, but hadn't I just named him? The kids began to whisper while my armpits became sticky. It was only a dumb game, but I felt like my honor was at stake.

"Time's up!" Mr. A. announced, sounding more cheerful.

I licked my lips and shrugged. "Hank Greenberg *again?*"

"Correct!" Mr. A. slapped his head lightly, like he couldn't believe I'd figured out his trick question.

To my right, a single pair of hands applauded—Geneva's hands. I bowed at her and laughed. She grinned back at me. "Where'd you learn so much about baseball?"

"My brother's baseball card collection. He's a real fanatic. He's studying communications at college now so he can be a sportswriter."

"Yeah, but you remembered *everything!* You really ticked off the guys."

We both laughed. "I have a pretty good memory," I admitted. "I can remember all kinds of useless stuff."

"Andi, do you want to pick another category?" Mr. A. asked glumly, interrupting our conversation.

Knowing about baseball was cool; knowing Bible facts, well . . . I decided to stop while I was ahead. "I think I'll pass," I told him.

Geneva was still smiling, which gave me the courage to ask her a question. "Where'd you get all those terrific bracelets?"

"This one's from Cancún," she began, fingering a tortoiseshell band, "and this one's from Morocco." She flashed a smile as she slipped off a leather bangle with tiny silver bells hanging from it. "Here, want to wear it?"

I may have hesitated a second before I put my hand through the bracelet. Before we became magically linked.

3

The Jewish New Year, Rosh Hashanah, is a time when people who haven't been to temple all year long show up at services. I guess it's because each new year brings you another shot at being a better person.

When I was little, I used to make the same resolution each September (or October, depending on where the holiday fell): to stop fighting with Mitchell. I think he made the same one, too, because during the first week, we'd be really nice to each other. I'd let him sit up front in the car whenever Ma drove us someplace, and I wouldn't complain when he ate the potato chips off my plate at Friendly's. And every night, he'd let me feed his pet goldfish, Gonzo.

But by the second week, riding in the backseat would start making me nauseous again, and I'd want the potato chips all to myself. Then Mitchell would complain that I was overfeeding Gonzo and take the little shaker of fish food back into his room.

This year, I hadn't settled on a single resolution. I'd

thought about it a lot, though. On some days, I'd vow not to let anything about me change, even if everyone and everything around me seemed to be changing. On others, I would've gladly volunteered to undergo the first personality transplant.

Since Hillside Community Temple is a pretty small place, the holiday services are held in a giant tent they erect just to fit in all the once-a-year worshipers. Inside are rows and rows of folding chairs that face a raised platform where the rabbi stands. Long strings of lights run across the top of the canopy, and waxy green plants hang from the structural poles. When the sun shines, you can see the shadows of autumn leaves dance across the canvas roof. At night the lights glow and wink like miniature constellations. Either way, the tent makes me feel a special connection to the universe. Like I'm miles from civilization, even though we're right next door to the synagogue and houses and street lamps and stuff.

I followed my parents through an open tent flap and scanned the rows for empty seats while they chatted with friends they hadn't seen in a while. The muscles of my stomach knotted as I was reminded that we'd only need three chairs this year. Mitchell hadn't come home from Penn State for the holidays. I closed my eyes and recalled the night he'd first told Ma his plan to stay at school.

It was this past Monday, after dinner, and I was up in my room reading *The Language of Goldfish* when the phone rang. My mother was still down in the kitchen, and we both picked up at the same time. "Hello?" she asked, a half beat ahead of me.

"Ma, it's Mitch." My brother sounded awfully quiet, tired maybe.

"It's about time you called. Haven't those dim-witted roommates of yours been giving you my messages? I've been trying to reach you for a week!"

"They're not dim-witted. I've been busy, that's all. How are Dad and Andi?"

In the background, I could hear water running. I knew Ma was scrubbing the dinner dishes while she held the receiver between her raised-up right shoulder and her ear. When she was through, she'd load them into the dishwasher to be washed again. You could always tell what kind of mood she was in by the way she worked. When she went into a cleaning frenzy, it was a good idea to stay out of her way.

"They're fine. And just in case you're still interested, I'm fine, too. How is school?"

"Okay." Sometimes it was hard to believe Mitch wanted to major in communications.

"I hope you're getting enough rest. Your father and I tried to call you at ten o'clock on Sunday night, and no one was home."

"Yeah, don't worry. Look, Ma, I'm sorry to have to tell you this, but . . ."

"What's the matter? I suppose you're out of money again. If you'd move back into the dorm, you wouldn't be spending so much on food. And I could do your laundry. I get sick just thinking about all those quarters you waste in the launderette!"

I imagined my mother, dishrag in hand now, furiously

14

swiping at a spot on her immaculate kitchen counter while she scolded my brother. And I could almost see Mitchell at the other end of the line, holding the phone at arm's length, waiting for the lecture to be over. I knew I should quit eavesdropping and hang up, but I was curious about what he was going to say. I missed him, even though his visits always turned our house into a war zone.

When Mitch first announced that he wanted to move out of the dorms and into an apartment with some of his friends, Ma went bonkers. Where was he going to find a quiet place to study? Who was going to see that he ate balanced meals? How was he going to keep the place clean? The place was probably full of roaches! But he went ahead and moved anyway. He found a part-time job at a gas station to help him cover the extra cost of rent and food. And even though he'd been living off campus since February, Ma was still carrying on about it.

"I don't need money, Ma. I'm calling to wish you a happy Rosh Hashanah, that's all."

My mother's voice softened just a little. "Well, that's very nice, but you might as well have saved yourself the price of a call. You'll be home on Friday."

Ten seconds of Mitchell's silence told me everything I needed to know. "No, I won't, Ma. I can't make it. I've got to work at the station this weekend."

"Don't be ridiculous. You can't miss the holiday for that nothing job of yours." I recognized the clink of glassware in the background, and I knew Ma was lining up the little bottles on her spice shelf like a platoon of soldiers. It was always the last thing she did before she considered the job of kitchen cleaning done. "You're running up your phone bill. I'll see you in time for dinner, Friday." Her voice was firm. "I'm making your favorite, apricot chicken."

"Ma, listen!" Mitchell had begun to shout. "I'm not coming home. I'll go to services here."

"Now you listen to me," my mother shrieked in a voice that made me want to hide under my bed. "Ever since you moved in with those worthless friends of yours, you've turned into a stranger! Don't you expect us to continue paying your bills if you're not going to show us proper respect!"

"You don't want respect, Ma, you want to run my life! I'm not going to let you."

"Howard! Howard, come talk some sense into your son!" On the other end, my brother was coolly silent. Was he still there? I wanted to shout at him, "Mitch, what about me? Can't you just put up with Ma for my sake? Don't you even care?" I bit my lips so hard that tears formed in the corners of my eyes. Before my father could come to the phone, Mitchell hung up.

"There are three seats in that row."

The sound of my mother's voice brought me back to the present. I opened my eyes and saw Geneva sitting in a back row of the tent. Her black hair shimmered in a shaft of sunlight, and her green eyes appeared nearly translucent. When she looked up and caught me studying her, I blushed hotly. She just smiled and patted the empty chair next to her. I was kind of surprised but pleased, too. "I'm going to sit with my friend. I'll see you later,"

I told my mother and father. I left before they could object.

There were two unoccupied chairs next to Geneva. I wondered if maybe I'd misunderstood her gesture. "Hi. These aren't your parents' seats, are they?" I asked, feeling suddenly dumb.

She smiled in a friendly way. "Don't be a dork. Have a seat. My parents are in Rome."

"Your parents left you home alone?" I squeaked as I plopped down. Two old ladies sitting in front of us turned to stare. When they moved, I caught a whiff of mothballs. I lowered my voice. "Sorry."

Geneva waved a hand in front of her nose as if to clear the air. "They offered to take me, but I didn't want to go. I've already been to Rome three times. My father's a troubleshooter for Skytrain Airlines."

I wasn't sure what a troubleshooter for an airline did, but I imagined it had something to do with hijackings and crashes and other serious stuff. My own father owned a wallpaper and paint store named Walloping Wallcoverings. "How'd you get here today?" I asked.

"My father arranged for our neighbors, the Chernovs, to bring me, so I wouldn't miss anything. At night I have to sleep at their house, too. They keep trying to feed me hamburgers for dinner, even though I've told them I'm a vegetarian." She rolled her eyes and shook her head dramatically.

"Oh." I was mildly disappointed. I'd already begun to imagine Geneva in her kitchen each night, whipping up weird meals.

"Shh!" the old ladies hissed at us. Rabbi Mandel,

dressed in a white prayer shawl, lumbered up the platform stairs like a great polar bear. He leaned on the podium, waiting, until the crowd fell silent.

"*L'shanah tovah*, my friends," he began, which means "Happy New Year" in Hebrew. His voice was more like a croak. "Welcome back to another new beginning at Hillside." He coughed into a handkerchief. "Although my spirit is eager for a new beginning, my body is not. Cold germs don't respect the holidays." There were affectionate chuckles all around. "So (*cough, cough, cough*) I have arranged for a younger and healthier body to take my place today (*cough, cough*)."

The congregation began murmuring as a tall, loose-limbed figure suddenly bounded out of the front row onto the platform and began pounding the rabbi's back. He wore a white prayer shawl, and his hair was pulled back Paul Revere style in a tight blond ponytail.

"I'd like to introduce you to our new rabbinic intern, Jeffrey Goodman," Rabbi Mandel said when he'd recovered his voice. "Many of you already know that Jeffrey is officially going to begin assisting me with services next month, although his chief responsibility will be as Hillside's director of youth activities."

Geneva and I looked at each other in astonishment. "What a hunk!" she whispered loudly.

Her words made me cringe, even though she was right. I wouldn't exactly have put it that way, but the new rabbi did look very young and *very* handsome. The old ladies twisted their necks and glared at us.

"Sorry," Geneva mumbled. But when they turned back around, we looked at each other again and burst out laughing. I pressed my face into my coat and pretended I was coughing. Geneva took the sleeve and wiped her eyes.

Rabbi Mandel began hacking again. When he was finished he said, "As you can see, I'm in no condition to conduct this morning's services. So Jeff has agreed to start his new job a bit early. Let's show him what Hillside hospitality is on this very special morning."

We opened our prayer books and followed along as the new rabbinic intern read. Up until then, the only kind of intern I'd ever heard of was the medical kind, like Doogie Howser. But Rabbi Jeff's deep, clear voice convinced me that he was the real thing. When he turned around to pray toward the cabinet that held the Torahs, or Bible scrolls, Geneva nudged me with her elbow. "Look at his yarmulke!"

A yarmulke is a small, round cap that Jewish men often wear during services to remind themselves that there's something higher than they are. I studied the one Rabbi Jeff had pinned to the back of his head, right above his ponytail. It was deep blue-black, like the night sky, with a swirl of tiny shooting stars crocheted in shiny gold thread. "Pretty cool," I had to admit.

Although the prayers continued, I began daydreaming about what Hillside would be like with a young guy like Jeffrey Goodman as director of youth activities. Maybe he'd give "rap" sermons . . . and call us "dudes" instead of "boys and girls" like Rabbi Mandel did . . . and organize trips to laser shows and rock concerts instead of to endless revivals of *Fiddler on the Roof.*

The service was over at noon. "Want to come home

with me?" Geneva asked as we followed the crowd out of the tent. "We could walk. It's really less than a mile."

This was an interesting proposition. After all, I was supposed to be improving myself for the new year. Maybe some of Geneva's sophistication would rub off on me. I wished Marci could see me now. Let her have Sharon Merrill!

I acted like I was thinking the invitation over. "Just let me tell my parents," I finally agreed. "I'll be right back."

"Walk?" my mother exclaimed when I found her. She made the word sound foreign and unhealthy.

I flapped my fists at my sides. "She says it's not far, Ma."

"It's cold today. You'll freeze." She waved a hand in the air like she was erasing any more thought of going to Geneva's.

"It's fifty-five degrees and I have a jacket."

"You didn't have lunch yet." My mother began walking toward the parking lot, where my father was getting our car. I had to chase after her while I continued arguing.

"I'm not hungry."

She stopped and faced me, arms crossed over her chest. "Who is this girl, anyway? You hardly know her."

"I already told you, she's in my Hebrew class. I want to go. You know I'm not exactly overloaded with friends right now, Ma."

My mother sighed deeply then, a sign she'd given in . . . almost. "All right. But your father and I will drop you off. That way we'll know where to pick you up later."

. . .

Geneva's house was old and roomy, with three levels if you counted the attic. I did, since that's where she had her room. It took up the whole top floor and was furnished just like an attic should be, with an iron bed, an old wardrobe, and a steamer trunk for her clothes and stuff. There was no desk, but I couldn't picture her doing homework anyway.

I thought of my own room: nine pieces of beige furniture designed to fit together. My mother and a store decorator had worked it all out. It was perfect—if you were a Bloomingdale's mannequin.

Geneva kicked off her shoes and sat cross-legged on the floor. Then she curled over until her forehead touched the rug, a woven concoction of different threads and fabrics in purples and golds that looked like it came from the same exotic lands as her bracelets. "This is my favorite yoga position," she explained. "It gets your blood flowing to your head. Very good for meditating. You should try it."

I sat down across from her on the floor and rolled my body forward, but my head didn't quite meet the rug. "I can't reach that far," I croaked.

"That's because you're not loosened up yet. You've got to keep practicing. Just let gravity pull you down."

"Okay." I forced myself over an inch farther, even though my shoulders were beginning to ache. I was determined to stay down there as long as Geneva did.

"So where do you go to school?" she asked. It was a weird position for a conversation.

If my face hadn't already been red from bending over, I would have blushed. "I used . . . to go . . . to Lazy Hollow . . . but this year . . . I'm at Barth."

"*The Barf Academy for the rich and selfish?* That's right here in my neighborhood. Why on earth would you want to go there?"

I gave in and sat up. My back was killing me. "My parents think the education's better," I told her.

"So is it?"

"Well, I've only been there a week. The classes are much smaller, and the kids are, um, different."

"In what way?"

I thought of Alana, Deidre, and Bonita carrying their lacrosse sticks through Barf's halls as if they were royal scepters. After the first day of school, they hadn't even glanced my way. I decided I didn't want Geneva to know what a loser they thought I was. "I don't know exactly. They seem so sure of themselves."

"You mean stuck-up?"

I started to laugh. "Yeah, that too. Anyway, I don't feel like I fit in very well." Boy, was that an understatement. I'd spent an entire week at Barf, and I was beginning to wonder if I'd ever make friends there. Twice Ms. Taylor had suggested I attend a meeting of the staff of *Barth Breezes*, the school literary journal, but so far I'd resisted. The last thing I wanted to do was get lumped together with the "Think Tanks" at Barf. Actually, I was considering trying out for the volleyball team next.

Geneva uncurled herself slowly and looked me in the eye. "Who cares? You should be your own person. Let them follow you."

"Yeah, maybe you're right." It was easy for her to say. She was sophisticated, gorgeous, and as flexible as a rubber band. I had a body like a ten-year-old boy, hair that frizzed like cotton candy—and a backache.

I glanced over to the barrel that served as her nightstand. On top there was a framed photo of a younger Geneva tucked in bed with a thin, frazzle-haired woman. A cake all lit up with candles sat in front of them on a tray.

"Who's that with you, your grandmother?"

"My mother. That was my ninth birthday . . . the year she died of cancer."

"I thought your parents were in Rome," I blurted out dumbly.

Geneva shrugged. "I meant my father and Claudia, his wife."

"Your stepmother."

"Technically, yes," she answered without looking at me.

I felt cautious and awkward, as if Geneva had entrusted me with a priceless vase or a piece of her grandmother's china that had to be handled with extreme care. I didn't know what I should say about the awful fact of her mother's death. Sure, life in my family wasn't perfect, but losing a parent was . . . irreversible. An image suddenly popped into my head of sweet, tragic Sara Crewe, the brave orphan in the book A Little Princess, which I still reread every time I stayed home sick from school. It was a weird thought, because I was certain Geneva would think that polite, obedient Sara was a real wimp.

"I'm really sorry about your mother," I murmured. "It must have been terrible. Is your stepmother nice?"

Geneva looked off toward the doorway. "If you like Barbie dolls." Then she rose from the floor in one smooth, graceful movement. "Let's eat! I'm starving. The Chernovs served *lamb chops* for dinner last night."

I followed her down to the kitchen and sat at the table while she poked through the refrigerator. She brought out an armful of jars and plates and set them down in front of me. "I'll just get us something to drink," she said, leaving me to examine the offerings.

There was a jar of large green olives and another with a label that read Marinated Artichoke Hearts. On one of the plastic-wrapped dishes a wedge of whitish cheese with thick green veins sat decomposing, while a second held a square of some liver-colored thing I couldn't name. I did recognize a half-eaten can of sardines, however.

"We've got mango and orange," Geneva said, returning to the table with two bottles and a box of crackers, "and we can use these for the cheese and the pâté."

"I'm not very hungry," I told her. "I think I'll just have some orange juice."

She looked up at me, surprised. "Are you sure? Sardines, artichokes, and olives make a great salad." She unscrewed the top of the olive jar and plucked one out. "My mother loved these. The two of us used to polish off an entire jar at a single sitting." She popped the olive in her mouth and pushed the jar toward me.

"No, really, I had a huge breakfast this morning."

Geneva seemed determined to feed me, though.

"Maybe you'd just like some ice cream. I think we've got chocolate chip."

"Okay, sure, I never turn down ice cream," I agreed, relieved that I wouldn't have to starve all afternoon.

She attacked the refrigerator once more and began rummaging through the freezer. "It's gone!" she announced indignantly after a minute. "Claudia must've finished it all before she went away."

"That's okay, I don't mind," I assured her.

But Geneva seemed genuinely disturbed. She stood in front of the open freezer with her hands on her hips and shook her head disapprovingly. "No, it wasn't right for her to eat it all."

Even though Claudia wasn't there, I had the uncomfortable feeling I'd wandered into a family fight. I wished Geneva would just drop the whole thing, but then that mysterious half smile took over her face. "I know! We'll go get some." She slammed the freezer door shut and snatched a set of keys off a hook on the kitchen wall. "My father left these."

They looked like car keys to me. "You mean drive?"

Her eyes took on a funny gleam. "Sure, why not? My dad always lets me drive the car in and out of the garage for him."

I felt my mouth tighten into the disapproving line my brother calls my "old-lady look." I tried to erase it before she noticed. "You don't have to worry about accidents in your garage, and besides, you have to be sixteen to drive." I hoped I sounded more calm than I felt.

Geneva played with the keys. "It isn't fair, I'm almost

fifteen! In Kansas, even fourteen-year-olds can get licenses." She flashed all her teeth at me. "Anyway," she cooed, "I could pass for sixteen."

I didn't mention the fact that I was still only thirteen. My birthday wasn't until December 31, almost three months away. "What if someone we know sees us? Or we're stopped by the police? Or we get a flat tire?" I asked quietly, but something inside me was already feeling light and free. Who would ever expect brainy, geeky Andi Applebaum to drive herself to town? My mother still tried to grab my hand when we crossed the street together!

"I think I'll get some double chocolate chunk," I announced.

4

acking out of the garage was no problem for Geneva. As she nosed the car easily down the street, I wondered how many times she'd done it before. Still, I did feel a little nervous when she took one hand off the wheel to turn on the radio. But I kept quiet and assigned myself the task of watching out for police cars and suspicious neighbors.

"Do you like new wave? This is the Junk Men," she told me, meaning the band we were listening to. "I have this album. Want me to copy it for you?"

"Sure," I agreed, although it was the weirdest music I'd ever heard. It reminded me of how our kitchen sounded one night last spring, when my brother and I'd dried the dishes together. It was Mitchell's idea to have a stacking contest with the pots and pans, and he'd managed to pile up nine of them before they collapsed and nearly gave my mother a breakdown. But no one touched the radio in our house except Ma, and her taste was even worse than this new-wave stuff. She listened to one of those stations that played dentist-office music: songs about little green apples and cakes left out in the rain.

Sometimes I thought about taking Mitchell's stereo into my room. He had a collection of tapes of old English groups like The Beatles and The Who that were nice, but I kind of preferred listening to them in his room. I liked to sit on his bed and look at his posters of football jerks. Sometimes I'd open his closet and find the place on the wall where I'd crayoned *Mitchell is a stupid head* when I was five. He'd never told our mother, and he'd never washed it off either.

Geneva hummed cheerfully while she drove. After a couple of minutes, I stopped feeling nervous and started to relax. In fact, I realized, I was actually enjoying myself. I felt like rolling down the window and waving to the public the way the president does. "I can't believe what a good driver you are!" I told Geneva.

She shrugged casually. "There's nothing to it." But from her smile, I could tell she was pleased with the compliment.

Since I didn't know the neighborhood, I wasn't surprised when she turned off onto a little side road. But then I caught a glimpse of a sign that said SANITATION YARD. "Hey, I thought we were going for ice cream!" I burst out.

Her eyes widened in surprise. "First you've got to learn how to drive, Andi," she answered, as if I were not thinking practically. The road opened onto a large black-topped lot with a line of garbage trucks parked at the far end. "This is a great place to practice. See, there's no one here but us and the flies." She turned off the ignition and faced me. "C'mon, let's change places."

Obediently, I got out of the car. I'd never done anything illegal before. There wasn't even a late library book in my life. For some reason, I thought of how Alana and her friends at Barf would look if they saw me behind the wheel. I got in beside Geneva. "Okay, shoot," I said.

She furrowed her brow and squinted. "First, turn the key until you hear the engine running. Good. Now just move the stick out of Park and into Drive." We lurched forward. "Give it a little gas, Andi. And you don't need to grip the steering wheel so tightly. You're going to get driver's cramp."

We jerked back and forth until we were both seasick. Finally, I gained enough confidence to keep a steady foot on the gas pedal, and we made wide turns around the lot. I remembered what a big deal Mitchell had made when he'd gotten his driver's license. Now I understood how he must have felt. It was like when the orthodontist takes your braces off . . . or the first day of summer vacation. I was free!

"This is incredible!" I shouted when I was sure I could talk and drive at the same time.

Geneva smiled and gave me the thumbs-up sign. Then she opened the glove compartment and pulled out a package of cigarettes.

I nearly hit a garbage truck. "I didn't know . . . I mean, I don't know anyone who smokes," I blurted out nervously as she removed one from the pack and held the car's lighter to the tip.

"This one is just to celebrate," she said between puffs. "Actually, these are my dad's. I'm trying to quit."

"Oh." I tried to appear flattered that she was smoking in my honor, but then I started to cough. "I'm allergic," I explained as the car began to jerk with each spasm.

She tossed the cigarette out the window and folded her arms behind her head. "It's okay. Now let's go get some ice cream. Onward, Jeeves."

Well, what was the sense of learning to drive if you couldn't go anywhere? I steered us over to the exit, feeling as though my body were possessed by a demonic new Andi. I wondered if soon my head would start spinning around three hundred and sixty degrees on my neck.

"Make a left. The shopping center is just straight ahead, about a mile down," Geneva directed.

As soon as I pulled out, I could see a car approaching us from the opposite direction. "What if the driver sees me? He'll know I'm not sixteen! We're going to get caught!" I began babbling. My palms got so sweaty, I was afraid they'd slip off the wheel. I was driving about five miles an hour.

Geneva found a pair of sunglasses in the glove compartment and arranged them on my face. She was perfectly cool, grinning even, like she was enjoying the possibility of getting caught. "There, now just act natural. You'd better speed up a little. It looks suspicious to be going so slowly."

I concentrated hard on staying in my lane and not throwing up. When we were almost face-to-face with the other driver, I saw it was an old woman, so short her eyes barely made it over the steering wheel. She looked at least ninety-five. Probably she wouldn't have noticed if a dog were driving Geneva's car.

"Turn there," Geneva said, pointing to the entrance of another parking lot.

I pulled in and stopped—jammed on the brakes, actually—so we both jerked forward like rag dolls. My parking wasn't too great either. The car was taking up about three spots, but fortunately the lot wasn't crowded. When I turned off the engine, I could feel my heart beating fast.

We crossed the parking lot to Yum Yum's. As soon as we entered, I realized what a big mistake we were making. Standing there licking a strawberry cone was Alana Voegel-Whitcroft, my guide at Barf.

"Hi, Andi!" Alana greeted me in her lazy voice. "Kenny and I are having ice cream for lunch. Aren't we too weird?" She nodded toward a table where Kenneth McKenna, a Barf boy I recognized, was hunched over a thick shake. When our eyes met, he raised an index finger as a greeting. Being more generous, I flashed my entire palm at him.

For a moment, I was startled. After my first day at Barf, Alana had completely ignored me, so I was surprised at how friendly she was acting now. She reminded me of Marci, who'd always been nice when we were alone, but who could be sarcastic and teasing when we were with other kids, especially Sharon Merrill.

"We're having ice cream for lunch, too," I told her, hoping I didn't sound as uncomfortable as I felt. "I guess that makes us weird also."

Alana's smile faded. It was okay for her to call herself

weird, but not for me to agree. "I didn't know you lived in Reed," she said.

"I don't. I'm visiting my friend." I nodded toward Geneva. "Geneva, meet Alana."

With a single glance, Alana took in Geneva, who was lounging against the counter, eyes half-closed with boredom. She was wearing a clingy purple sweater, a short black skirt, and boots, and her unruly hair was practically covering one eye. There was a challenge in her languid posture that I found satisfying.

"Where do you go to school?" Alana asked.

"Reed High." Geneva reached up and pushed her hair off her face. Her bracelets clinked and jingled.

"Why don't you two sit down over there with Kenny and me?" Alana offered. I guess she was curious, or maybe she just wanted something to discuss at lunch on Monday.

"We can't. We're in a hurry," I answered, flashing Geneva a look that said "Let's get out of here!" I turned my attention to the list of flavors.

"Oh. Well, see you in school then," Alana said coolly. "Nice to meet you, Geneva." She took a seat next to the silent hulk and whispered something in his ear.

After we got our cones, Geneva dangled the car keys conspicuously. "Andi, do you want to drive, or should I?" She didn't wait for me to answer. "Do either of you need a lift?" she called to Alana and Kenny. The hairs on the back of my neck stood up, and my teeth locked together.

Alana looked confused. "My mother is picking us up. What grade did you say you were in?"

"I didn't." Geneva linked her arm through mine and led me off. "Come on, Andi."

I could feel them watching us through the window as we crossed the parking lot. When we got to the car, Geneva swung the keys in front of my nose, but I shrugged them off and got in on the passenger side. The demon that had possessed me was gone. My hands were shaking—the same two hands that had steered us here.

Geneva climbed in beside me on the driver's side. "What's the matter?"

"Why'd you do that?" I asked, fighting to keep my voice even. "If they tell on us, we could be arrested or expelled or something!"

She snorted at the idea. "Relax, they won't tell. Anyway, I bet everyone at that snooty school of yours quits snubbing you now."

I stared hard through the windshield, wondering how I'd ever let myself get into this situation. Driving illegally with someone I barely knew . . . someone who was turning out to be unpredictable. I must've been temporarily insane!

Geneva dropped the keys into her lap and sighed loudly. "I thought you were having fun."

"I was . . . for a while. But I can't afford to get caught. I'm not like you."

As soon as I said the words, I realized what a mistake I'd made. Geneva's fine black eyebrows arched over her clear green eyes. "Oh, really?"

"I mean, you're more adventurous," I rushed to explain. "And independent." She seemed to be considering my words. Her shoulders relaxed a bit, which encouraged me to continue. "My parents . . . you don't know what they're like. If they found out about this, they'd never let me out of the house again."

After a moment she nodded as if she understood. "It's okay. I figured you'd want to impress those kids, that's all."

"I just don't know if I can trust them not to tell someone."

The annoyed look on Geneva's face had been replaced by a serious expression. "You're right. You can't trust too many people." She turned the key in the ignition, and the motor started up. "Come on. Let's get this thing back to my house."

5

I was amazed to hear Geneva's voice on the phone the next day. After my anxiety attack in the parking lot of Yum Yum's, I was sure she thought I was too much of a baby for her. But here she was on the line, offering me a second chance. This time I was determined not to blow it.

"I'm highlighting my hair today. Want to help?" she asked.

"Sure." I hadn't the slightest idea what highlighting black hair meant or how you did it. "What time should I come?"

"Anytime. Now if you can."

"Okay, I'll see if I can get a ride," I told her. "Bye."

My parents were a little surprised that I wanted to go to Geneva's again so soon, but they didn't put up much opposition. It was Sunday, there was no Hebrew school on account of the holiday, and I'd already finished my homework. I thought Dad would take me by himself, but Ma decided to come along too, "for the ride." Just before we left, I rummaged through the refrigerator for the leftover potato pancakes my mother had made the night before and put them in a bag to take along.

I rang the bell of the Peaces' big house and waited on the step. If my father had been standing next to me, he would've commented on how the paint was peeling around the door and windows. When Geneva didn't appear after a minute or two, I rang again. My parents were still in the car out front, just to be sure no one kidnapped me before I got inside. After my third ring, Geneva swung the door open. "Come on in, I'm on the phone," she said, disappearing back into the house. I waved to my mother and closed the door behind me.

Geneva's voice echoed from the kitchen. "*I know* I said I was coming to the meeting, Kate, but my father is taking me to that new movie about the whale civilization this afternoon."

Her father was back early? I stopped just outside the kitchen door and held my breath.

"No, that is not why I quit. . . . I already told you, I'm sorry I called you a bunch of wimps!"

I poked my head into the kitchen. When she saw me, Geneva held up a finger to indicate she'd be off in a minute. After a few more seconds, she rolled her eyes at me in disbelief.

"If you want to know the truth, Kate," she snapped into the receiver, "I think that petition Tanya drafted is pretty dumb. What does she mean 'For the rest of the semester, we females deserve an equal amount of time on the computers'? He owes us more than that!"

She made a yak-yak-yak motion with her hand to let me know Kate was a blabbermouth. "Listen," she said after a few more seconds, "I've got to go. My dad's in the car already. See you in school."

She hung up abruptly and grinned at me. "Kate is one of the wimps from math class. Our teacher, Mr. Harvey, is left over from the Stone Age, and he only lets boys use the computers. Of course, he says everyone will get a chance, but not one single girl has been picked yet. I said we should stage a protest by boycotting math class —but those girls are all chickens. They want to do something 'more acceptable' . . . like hand in a stupid petition."

"Yeah, that is pretty gutless," I agreed, although I knew boycotting math class was the same thing as cutting— which I'd never done. I held out the bag of potato pancakes. "I thought maybe the Chernovs served meatballs last night, so I brought you these."

She took it and examined the contents. "Mmm, thanks, but I didn't go. My dad and Claudia are coming home tonight, so I convinced Mrs. Chernov that I needed one evening alone to clean up." She rolled her eyes again. "Mrs. Chernov kept calling every five minutes to see if I was okay."

Actually, I couldn't help noticing that the house could use some cleaning up. There were dust balls as big as oranges in the corners of the kitchen, and when Geneva opened the refrigerator door to stow the pancakes, the sickly smell of spoiled food drifted out. I followed her upstairs, where a hill of dirty underwear rose outside the bathroom. But Geneva just kicked it aside and pushed the door open. "We'll do the henna in here."

"Henna. Didn't the Egyptians use that in cosmetics?" I asked, remembering something I'd read when we'd studied ancient civilizations in sixth grade.

She shrugged. "I doubt if the Egyptians had Lady Care-all. Anyway, this stuff gives your hair red highlights. It should look cool."

"Red highlights on black hair?"

"Sure, the native Hawaiians have them naturally."

Since I'd never been to Hawaii, I had to take her word for it. I picked up the Lady Care-all box and examined its picture of a smiling woman with red-glinting hair flared out around her like a shawl. If that was what henna did for you, Geneva had nothing to worry about. Then I turned the box over and found the directions, which were pretty simple. You just washed your hair and painted the stuff on evenly. Afterward, you dried your hair with a blow-dryer. According to Lady Care-all, the highlights would last six to eight weeks.

"Well, it looks easy," I said. "Wash your hair and I'll paint it on."

She turned on the faucet in the sink and leaned into the basin. "I thought about making myself a blond like Claudia," she told me as she lathered up her hair, "but I didn't want her to think I admired her or anything. Actually, with your light brown hair, you might want to try blond highlights."

"I don't think so," I said. "Then I'd look like the golden jock goddesses of Barf." I took an ordinary paintbrush and a can that looked like it could be filled with tuna out of the Lady Care-all box. "I need a nail file or something to pry the lid off this can."

"Look in that drawer on the left."

I found the nail file lying among items we didn't have at home: a package of extralong fake fingernails, a medieval torture instrument that Geneva said was an eyelash curler, a tube of "kissable" lip base, a crumpled, mostly empty package of cigarettes, several matchbooks, and something called "mole enhancer." Since Geneva didn't have any noticeable moles, I figured the stuff was Claudia's. I was beginning to wonder if Geneva's stepmother was like a middle-aged Madonna. Carefully, I worked the henna can open with the file. It was filled with a gloppy brown gel. "I think it needs to be stirred," I told Geneva.

She grabbed a toothbrush out of a holder on the side of the sink. "Here, use this."

"Your toothbrush?" I asked skeptically.

"No, Claudia's." In the mirror above the sink she caught my horrified expression. "Go ahead! I already used it last night to scrub some nail polish off the sink."

I closed my eyes and plunged the toothbrush into the brownish goo while Geneva wound a towel around her hair and squeezed out the excess moisture. While I stirred, she found a comb that was missing several teeth and pulled it through her hair. "Okay, I'm ready," she said, addressing my reflected image again.

"What should I do with this?" I held up the toothbrush. Geneva pointed to the garbage. I flung it in, wondering what condition Claudia's teeth were in.

Geneva draped the towel around her shoulders, and I

began painting her hair. I was a little nervous. What if she hated how it came out? "Did you ever highlight your hair before?" I asked.

"Sure. Last spring I used this hot pink spray on a few strands in the front. It looked really cool, too, but when the dean at school saw it, he sent me home to wash it out."

"Was your father mad?" In my brother's senior year of high school, he'd come home from a friend's house one afternoon with his ear pierced. First, my mother nearly had a heart attack. Then she'd practically killed Mitchell, pulling at the little hoop in his freshly punctured ear while she screamed at him.

"No, why should he be?" Geneva made it sound like a challenge.

I brushed the gel over the ends of her hair while I thought. "My mother expects me to look . . . proper," I answered uncomfortably. "She's got this thing about respect."

"Do you always do what your mother says?"

Our eyes met in the mirror. "Your hair's done," I told her. "Let's dry it."

She sat on the hamper while I stood over her with the dryer. It was hard to believe the murky gel was going to dry into glowing red highlights, but I turned the gadget on high and began working. The thing was too noisy to talk over, which was fine with me. The first to dry were the ends. As soon as I looked at them, I knew there was something wrong.

"How's it look?" she shouted.

"Different . . . interesting," I answered, feeling like a boulder had just dropped into my stomach.

"Really? Is there a lot of red?"

"Well, not exactly," I mumbled. As Geneva's hair dried, she was getting highlights, only they weren't red.

She turned to face me. "What do you mean?"

I shut off the dryer. "It looks . . . it's sort of . . . I mean, it's kind of . . . almost . . . purple."

She jumped up and swept the hair forward over her right shoulder. Staring in the mirror, she examined the purple-hued black hair, which looked iridescent, like the feathers of a blackbird. Then she broke out into a big grin.

"It's gorgeous! I love it!"

My knees felt weak. I collapsed on the hamper. "You do?"

"Absolutely. I can't wait till my dad sees it!"

"What about school?" I asked. "Do you think the dean will have you suspended? According to the box, this stuff lasts about eight weeks."

"Nah, they try very hard not to fail me."

I wondered about her answer, but I didn't ask any more questions. After I'd finished drying her hair, Geneva said, "Now it's your turn."

"No, thanks. My mother would shave my head if I came home with purple hair."

"Well, I have to do *something* for you today," she insisted.

Nervously, I began backing out of the bathroom. "No, you don't. Really. I like being boring."

But she grabbed me by the wrist. "I know something we can do that your mother won't even notice."

I stopped pulling away. "What?"

"We can make you a wish braid." When I looked puzzled, she held her hair up off her neckline and exposed a tiny tightly braided strand that was wrapped with purple and red thread. "See? When my hair's down, you can't even see it, but it's neat 'cause it never comes out. After you sleep on it a few nights, the hairs kind of fuse together because it's so tight. The only way to undo it is to cut it off."

"Why would you want one if you can't see it?" I asked.

"Because it represents your deepest, most secret wish. You cut it off when the wish comes true. Kind of like a sacrifice."

"Oh." The idea sort of appealed to me. Not the sacrifice part, but the thought of having a secret hidden under my hair that my mother couldn't criticize—or even see.

I held up my hair and pulled a small lock down from underneath. "Okay," I said determinedly, "go ahead."

I was curious about what her wish braid represented, but she didn't say, and I knew better than to pry.

6

The following Sunday, Rabbi Jeffrey Goodman stood in front of the class, rocking on the heels of his running shoes. His thumbs were hooked in the belt loops of his blue jeans, and his smile was warm and easy. *"Tikkun olam!"* he announced. "It means 'to repair the world.' That's what we're going to try to do in this class, beginning right now."

"We're supposed to be working on symbolism in ceremonies this month," Matt Gruenwald informed him. I knew Matt wasn't the least bit interested in symbolism or ceremonies, but he did enjoy needling teachers.

"Forget about that! We've got the work of the righteous to do."

We gave each other looks that said "Huh?" but our new teacher kept on talking. "First, I've got to get to know all of you. We'll start by having you tell me what you think are the biggest problems in the world."

It sounded kind of crazy, but I could see the sense in it, too. Knowing what someone thinks is a problem can tell you a lot about him or her. Like last year, Marci used to worry about who was having a party and hadn't invited her, or whether she'd be nominated for membership in the Key Club, which was supposed to be based on the three A's: attendance, achievement, and "attitude." She'd even expected me to worry about those things. Sometimes I did, but usually I'd been more concerned about the next day's math test, or the next week's Shakespeare paper, or whether my mother was going to find the book of chest exercises I'd bought at a store in town called The Exershop.

"The Mets' left-handed pitching!" Jordan Daniels didn't wait to be called on. His answer confirmed what I'd known all along: He was a jerk.

Our ponytailed rabbinic intern didn't even flinch. "C'mon, you all see newspapers and television. Try again."

While my brain was still searching last night's news for an answer that would impress him, Geneva flicked her ringleted wrist. "Homelessness," she announced, accompanied by a racket of bells and clinks.

"Ding! Ding! Ding! One point for Miss Bojangles!" Rabbi Jeff sprang up and wrote *homelessness* on the chalkboard. I saw he was wearing a different yarmulke: black and yellow, with the Batman logo crocheted into it. "Your name, Miss Bojangles?"

"Geneva Peace." She flashed him her Mona Lisa smile.

Rabbi Jeff whistled through his teeth, which I think is extremely masculine. "Great name! Are your parents some kind of peace activists?"

That brought a round of snickering from my classmates, who, naturally, didn't know that Geneva is the international city of peace, former home of the League of Nations (which no longer exists), birthplace of the Geneva Conventions (a series of treaties that protect prisoners and wounded people during wartime), and currently the European headquarters of the United Nations. Knowing all that stuff was okay for Knowledge Bowl, but not so good in real life, so I didn't volunteer the information.

Anyway, the class's laughter didn't bother Geneva a bit. She stretched lazily, as if she had just awakened, and shook out her purplish mane. "Actually, Geneva is my father's favorite city. He travels a lot."

Rabbi Jeff rested his eyes on her for a few seconds before he turned his attention back to world problems. "Okay, I need an answer from someone else."

"Drugs," Samantha Schaeffer cooed. Her black eyelashes fluttered over her wide eyes.

"Excellent!" Rabbi Jeff crowed approvingly. "And you are . . . ?"

"Samantha Schaeffer." Sam's smile was disgustingly coy in her bright red lipstick. Her sweater matched the color perfectly. Last year, her favorite color had been frosted pink and she'd worn lots of pink clothes.

"I'm Karen! AIDS!" Karen Harper trilled next.

"Karen *AIDS?*" our new teacher teased. We all laughed, even Karen. "Actually, AIDS is very serious business," Rabbi Jeff said, turning sober. He added it to the chalkboard list.

"Nuclear weapons. I'm Leah," Leah Cole said shyly.

"Hi, Leah." Rabbi Jeff's smile made her blush deeply. He scratched *nuclear weapons* on the board, too.

I waited until he'd finished writing and was facing the class again. "The thinning of our ozone layer. The greenhouse effect. Acid rain," I offered, keeping my voice low and cool. "I'm Andi Applebaum."

"Ah, Andi. I believe I've found the class scientist and crusader," Rabbi Jeff teased, clasping both hands over his heart. I sank down in my seat.

"May I be excused? I think I'm going to toss my whole-grain cookies," Matt Gruenwald called out. But then he said, "Landfills, the biodegradable plastics hoax, the whole mentality of the disposable age." And the funny thing was, he glanced at me when he spoke, not our new rabbinic intern.

"And you are . . . ?"

"Matt Gruenwald."

Rabbi Jeff wiggled his eyebrows. "Maybe we could put you and Andi in a category together. We could call it something like *environmental destruction*."

The class laughed and I joined in, although I wasn't sure I wanted to be lumped together with Matt.

"Rabbi Doctor? Don't forget hunger," Jordan yelled out. He couldn't deal for too long with not being the center of attention. When we turned to look at him, he grabbed his stomach and groaned, "I'm starving."

"Rabbi Doctor?" There was skepticism in Rabbi Jeff's voice.

"Sure, it's like another name for a rabbinic intern," Jordan said, all innocence.

This time Rabbi Jeff grabbed his own stomach. "Ooh, that's bad. Why don't you just call me R.J., and I'll call you . . . wise guy."

We continued around the room until everyone had made a suggestion. Mark Silverstein, who never smiled, offered "The deficit." And Ben and Brad Tamir, our resident twins, came up with a two-headed answer, "Terrorism."

"Okay, now we've got an agenda!" Rabbi Jeff gave the chalkboard a satisfying smack.

I studied the list, which was headed *The World According to Grades 8 & 9*:

> homelessness
> drugs
> AIDS
> nuclear weapons
> environmental destruction
> hunger
> the deficit
> terrorism

Agenda? The whole thing was ridiculous. How could ten teenagers and a hippie rabbi do anything about even one of those, when entire governments had tried and failed? We might as well be playing Hebrew "Jeopardy!" with Mr. Aronson.

7

*M*att was on my wavelength. "Yeah, sure, we're really going to save the world," he grumbled, just loud enough for everyone—including the rabbi—to hear.

Very slowly, Rabbi Jeff walked over to Matt and rested a hand on each of his shoulders. No one breathed. "You weren't listening," he said quietly. "I said *tikkun olam* meant 'to repair the world,' which can be done by helping just one person at a time. That is, if you want to. *Do you?*"

"Yeah, well, sure," Matt stammered.

Who could say no?

"At a Save Our Planet rally in the city I got this button that said Think Globally, Act Locally. Isn't that kind of what you mean?" Geneva asked.

"Exactly!" Rabbi Jeff smiled at her in a way that made me wish I'd thought of something equally relevant to say. But it seemed that all I knew was a bunch of boring facts, like the names of the states that make up the Delmarva peninsula and how many people there are in Japan. You couldn't save the world with those facts.

Rabbi Jeff turned his attention back to the rest of us. "All the years you've been coming here, your teachers have stressed the importance of *tzedakah*—doing the right thing; giving charity. Now's your chance to put what you've learned into action. Some friends of mine have been running a soup kitchen in the city called Heavenly Vittles. They're planning to serve turkey dinners to anyone who shows up on Thanksgiving Day: the hungry, the homeless, and lots of other folks who are down on their luck. Most of the paid staff will be off on Thanksgiving, so Heavenly Vittles needs volunteers to help with the cooking, serving, and cleaning. I've signed on, and I've promised to bring as many of you to help as I can."

A wonderful picture arose before me. There was Rabbi Jeff, sleeves rolled up, his muscular arms carving mountains of turkey. And I was right beside him, handing out heaping platefuls to a sea of grateful faces. I would be tireless, a pillar of strength, a living Statue of Liberty. My heart soared . . . until the vision was replaced by another image: my parents when I told them that instead of being home for Thanksgiving dinner, I'd be spending my day at a soup kitchen. My mother would throw down her dish towel and faint on her spotless linoleum floor, while my father would go upstairs to his room and shut the door.

"What about our families? My parents are expecting me to have Thanksgiving dinner with them," I blurted out. Some of my classmates began nodding and murmuring, too.

"No problem. We'll be driving down in my van around six A.M. and returning by two. You'll be back in plenty of time for Mom's stuffing." He picked up a sheaf of papers from his desk and began passing them out. "I've photocopied a whole bunch of articles about hunger in America for us to read together. It's important to understand something about the people you'll be meeting before we actually go to Heavenly Vittles. Next week I'll pass out permission slips for you to bring home to your parents."

If he had known my parents, he might have given up right then. I was trying to think of a way even to approach the subject without making my mother hysterical when Geneva turned to me, green eyes shining. "This class is going to be so cool!" she purred.

"Yeah, I know," I agreed, although to myself I added, *for you.* I couldn't help thinking that there didn't seem to be anyone to stand in her way, and a sense of envy welled up inside me. Geneva's lack of parental supervision seemed almost appealing. But the feeling was immediately replaced by a wave of guilt. Of course, I didn't want anything to happen to my own mother. I just wished she'd give me a little space sometimes.

• • •

Actually, so far Geneva had turned out to be pretty good at predicting my future. At least, she'd been right about the kids at Barf not snubbing me anymore. On the Monday following my drive to Yum Yum's, Alana Voegel-Whitcroft had actually invited me to sit with her and her friends in the cafeteria. Since I usually sat alone, I couldn't think of a convincing excuse to turn her down.

"Come sit over here between Dickerson and me," she

cooed as I approached her table with my tray. Alana and her group called each other by their last names. Bonita Dickerson sat in front of me in French, but she never even said *bonjour*. Now she smiled brightly and slid over to let me in. "Hi, Applebomb." I couldn't tell if she was mispronouncing my name on purpose (the *a-u-m* in *Applebaum* should almost rhyme with *town*) or if she thought she was saying it correctly. Her conversational French wasn't too terrific either.

"You already know Van Dorne," Alana said, grinning at the girl who'd called my Penn State sweatshirt "sweet." I hadn't worn it to school since then. "And these two are Tittle and Porter." She nodded at the girls who were sitting across the table. Actually, I recognized them; Barf wasn't that big. Privately, I'd named them The Two Muses, since they both had blond hair, long necks, and milky skin like the goddesses in Greek mythology, and they always traveled the halls together.

"Voegel-Whitcroft said she and Kenny ran into you at Yum Yum's this weekend," Deidre Van Dorne announced, smiling slightly. "Do you dri—ah, get over there often?" Obviously, Alana had told her about the car.

"Not really." Why let on that it was my first—and only—time?

Caroline Tittle's eyes went wide. "Kenny McKenna? You went with *him*?" she squealed at Alana.

Alana shrugged. "I was bored. There's nothing to do in Reed on Saturdays." She smiled at me conspiratorially. "Unless you can drive."

"Why don't we have a beauty session at my house next

51

Friday night?" Bonita suggested. "We'll do manicures, pedicures, face masks, mustache waxes—the works. You can all sleep over."

She looked right at me when she spoke, so I knew I'd been included. The invitation made me very uncomfortable. Just because I'd driven a car, they thought I was a wild, daring, *fun* person.

"I don't think I can," Phoebe Porter said, saving me from having to answer right away. "There's a meeting of the *Barth Breezes* staff after school Friday, and I'm on the art committee. We usually stay pretty late. Plus, I'm having a big English test Monday, so I'll have a lot of studying to do that weekend."

I was surprised to hear that Phoebe worked on the literary magazine. My homeroom teacher, Ms. Taylor, had tried to get me to attend the last meeting, but I'd made up some excuse about a dentist appointment after school. Maybe I wasn't going to be the school athlete, but I didn't want to be the school Shakespeare either. I'd forgotten about the English test, however, and since Phoebe and I were in the same class, I now had an excuse to get out of going to the beauty session. I turned to Phoebe. "Yeah, that test is going to be really tough. I've got to study, too."

"Then you two can work together at Dickerson's," Alana said. "Applebomb's smart. It's a sure A for you, Porter."

Phoebe smiled at me shyly. "Well, *Julius Caesar* is kind of confusing. Would you mind, Andi?"

She seemed nice, too quiet maybe, but my first few

52

weeks at Barf had been pretty lonely. I was tempted to accept the invitation. Still, I wasn't ready to spend the night with the Barfettes. Besides, I bit my fingernails and picked my toenails, so manicures and pedicures were out. And what if they expected me to drive over?

"I can't that night. I'm going to a special youth service at my temple." It was true about the service, though I hadn't decided to go until that moment. "But I can help you with English during study hall on Friday if you want," I offered.

"Okay, thanks," Phoebe agreed quickly. It almost seemed as if she was relieved to get out of going to Bonita's, too.

It was only a study date, but for the first time at Barf, I felt hopeful.

8

*T*he next Sunday, while we were sitting in Rabbi Jeff's class, waiting for him to set up a videotape about the nuclear accident in Chernobyl, I told Geneva about my lunch with Alana and her friends. I thought she'd be amused at how impressed they were by our drive to Yum Yum's. Instead, a look of distaste crossed her face.

"You ate lunch with *them?*" she asked incredulously.

I shrugged and picked at some lint on my sleeve. "Well, yeah. I've been eating lunch by myself for three weeks. I'm getting kind of bored with my own company."

"What else have you been doing with them?" Her voice was strangely tight.

"Nothing. I—"

"I suppose now you're going to start playing lacrosse or field hockey or something."

"No!" I protested, wondering why I suddenly felt guilty.

"Do they call you on the phone for homework and stuff?"

"*No!* We just ate lunch together." I didn't mention the study date with Phoebe.

Holding her neck and shoulders stiff, Geneva shifted a half turn away from me. "I like to sit alone at lunch," she announced, in a voice that could give you frostbite.

I wondered why she was so irritated. Wasn't it my business if I wanted to eat with snobs and creeps? "I guess I'm not as interesting as you," I said, making a stab at humor. "I need . . . acquaintances." I was going to say friends, but I changed my mind.

"I have friends," she snapped. "Lots of them."

"Well, sure," I answered. But I couldn't help remembering the phone call I'd overheard between Geneva and her classmate Kate.

"So, what did your stuck-up friends say about our drive?" Geneva asked over her shoulder.

"They think I'm secretly a party animal. What a riot! They actually invited me over on Friday night."

She turned toward me again and eyed me coolly. "Oh?"

"I told them I'm going to the youth service on Friday night," I added hurriedly. "Do you want to come with me?"

She turned a bangle around her wrist. "Well, Kate and some of the other kids at school asked me to go ice-skating with them . . . although I think spinning around in circles all night is really lame."

I love to ice-skate, but I didn't say so. "According to the temple bulletin board, Rabbi Jeff is conducting the service on Friday night. You could come over for dinner first and help convince my parents to let me go down to

Heavenly Vittles on Thanksgiving." I knew that if I asked her to watch R.J. do his laundry, she couldn't resist.

"Well, okay. I'll just tell Kate I'm busy."

. . .

On Friday night, I circled the dining-room table, inhaling the rich aromas of my mother's cooking. Earlier in the week, I'd told her that Geneva was a vegetarian, but she'd only shrugged and answered, "Girls your age need meat." It didn't matter anyway. Even without the pot roast, there was enough food under the heavy covered bowls and platters to fill anyone up: homemade cream of mushroom soup; noodle kugel (a sweet, cheesy pasta casserole); cranberry-pecan relish; broccoli and cauliflower in cheddar sauce; sour pickles and tomatoes; and challah, the traditional Jewish bread served on Friday nights.

I began to worry that maybe my mother had cooked too much. One day of our family's leftovers could probably feed a whole village in some countries. We'd discussed the world food shortage last year in my social studies class, and the teacher had pointed out that if farmers didn't have to grow feed for cattle, there'd be more room to grow food for people. I wondered if Geneva was a vegetarian for moral reasons.

But it wasn't just the food that was worrying me. All week, I'd had visions of my mother pushing Geneva's purplish hair off her face, clucking over her armful of bracelets, and telling "true stories" about what happened to girls who smoked cigarettes . . . or wore their jeans too tight . . . or didn't listen to their mother's advice.

Marci had been used to Ma, but I didn't think Geneva

would appreciate her lectures. What's more, Geneva was likely to say whatever was on her mind, and my mother didn't put up with back talk.

By the time the doorbell rang, I was such a wreck that I was amazed to see Geneva smiling. She was dressed in a black turtleneck, a gauzy pink skirt, and black spandex leggings. Her hair was pulled up neatly in a pink elastic band so you could hardly see the purple streaks, and there were silver bells hanging from her ears. "You look great!" I told her.

"Thanks." Her face shone like it had just been scrubbed.

I took a deep breath and led her into the dining room, where my parents were waiting. "Ma, Dad, Geneva's here."

"I think we can see that," my father teased.

"Sit down over here," my mother said, pulling out a chair. "We're looking forward to getting to know you better."

Right away I lost my appetite. If Ma managed to learn much about Geneva, I might as well forget about seeing her again. Even worse, after an evening of my mother's questions, Geneva might never want to see *me* again.

Geneva surveyed the table wide-eyed and turned to my mother. "It smells heavenly, Mrs. Applebaum! Do you always eat like this?"

"Not since Mitchell left," my mother answered solemnly. "This is the first time we've had someone sitting in his chair."

Ever since Mitchell had moved into his apartment,

Ma talked about him as if he were dead. And in a way, it felt like he was, because I never got to see him. Ma was wild with anger. She made Dad give Mitch an ultimatum: Come home once a month or pay your own tuition next year. So in order to save money, my brother worked more hours at the station. It gave him one more excuse for not coming home.

Once over the summer when Ma and Dad were out, I'd called to see if I could talk him into coming home for a visit. "You don't know how it feels to be out of there, Andi," he'd replied. "Like being let out of one of those plastic bubbles that kids who don't have any antibodies live in. I eat junk food anytime I want, I wear my socks three days in a row if I feel like it, and my room smells like it belongs to a real person instead of Mr. Clean. But when I come home, they treat me like a little kid again. They want to know where I'm going and when I'm coming home. Sometimes I don't even know the answer to those questions. I have to lie, just to get them off my back!"

After that conversation, I'd spent a lot of time thinking. Sure, my parents were overprotective, so why didn't I feel as stifled as Mitchell? It wasn't that I was a spineless goody-goody really, it was just that I hated all the fighting. When Mitchell was home, it had been my job to cheer everyone up after an argument. I'd sing, tell jokes, bestow pats and kisses—anything—to make us a happy family again. It was exhausting. Besides, if I argued with my parents, who would play the peacemaker?

Geneva gave me a sidelong glance but didn't ask any

questions. Instead, she wolfed down her cream of mushroom soup. "That was incredibly delicious!" she said enthusiastically. "My stomach is in heaven."

"Maybe you'd like to bring the recipe home?" Ma offered. Her mouth was smiling, but I couldn't help noticing how her eyes shifted down Geneva's armful of bracelets to her purple-polished nails.

"Oh, Claudia doesn't cook." To my surprise, Geneva popped a forkful of pot roast into her mouth next. She must have forgotten that she was a vegetarian. "Mmm," she crowed. "I feel like I'm back in old Russia."

Both my parents burst out laughing. I squirmed with embarrassment for Geneva, but she seemed to actually be enjoying the attention.

"Sweetheart, in old Russia the only thing on the table would have been potatoes!" my father told her.

"That reminds me of the time I was in Scotland," Geneva said, fork in midair. "The food was so awful, I *lived* on potatoes. Their national dish is called haggis. Do you know what that is?"

"What?" I asked, trying to get in on the conversation.

"A stew made from the heart, lungs, liver, and stomach of a sheep," Geneva answered before she shoveled another bite of pot roast into her mouth.

I looked at the chunk of beef I'd speared onto my own fork and put it down. "Sorry I asked."

"You think that's bad? In Manila I ate jellied pigeon blood before I realized it wasn't black cherry Jell-O." She looked up from her plate at me. "Believe it or not, it wasn't bad."

"Oh." Suddenly I wished the jellied cranberry relish on my plate would disappear. I reached for a nice, safe pickle.

"In Korea, they pickle everything," Geneva announced, just as I was about to take a bite. "Cabbage, carrots, spinach, sprouts, and lots of stuff you wouldn't recognize. They call it kimchi. It all gets chopped up with this big cleaver, you know? One time a friend of my father took us to a restaurant in Seoul, and the waitress brought a jar of kimchi to our table, and there was a finger floating in it." Her eyes went wide as if she were seeing a finger in Ma's pickle bowl. "When we told the waitress, she just fished it out of the jar."

I dropped the pickle on my plate, uneaten. "I'd rather starve to death than eat that stuff," I said.

Geneva shrugged and kept on eating. "When you've traveled as much as I have, Andi, you learn to handle things."

In spite of the fact that she was probably right, my feelings were a little hurt. I wished she'd stop showing off how worldly she was. I was thinking maybe she didn't realize how she sounded, when she began slathering Ma's homemade red horseradish on a slice of challah.

"Geneva, dear, that's very hot," Ma cautioned. "We only use a little dab." She flashed a satisfied smile at my father that I knew meant "This girl may know a lot about foreign cuisine, but she obviously hasn't had a home-cooked Jewish meal."

"Oh, that's okay," Geneva answered matter-of-factly. "I'm used to hot foods. When we were in Thailand, my father challenged me to a hot-pepper-eating contest. I won, but I couldn't taste anything for days afterward." She took a big bite of the reddened bread and smiled brightly at my mother, full mouth and all.

Ma got kind of red herself. She began rearranging the serving dishes. "Well, you certainly have been a lot of places," she observed, as she moved the broccoli and cauliflower to where the pickles and tomatoes were and vice versa. "Do your parents travel for business or pleasure?"

When I was ten, Ma had bought me the first six volumes of the Nancy Drew detective series for my birthday, because she'd adored reading them herself when she was a kid. Maybe that's how she got to like poking around in other people's business so much. Too bad she hadn't been hooked on a different series—something harmless like Doctor Dolittle.

Geneva didn't seem to mind being interrogated, though. "My father's a troubleshooter for Skytrain Airlines," she explained. "Those trips were all business, except for Paris. Now *there* the food was great! I ate chocolate mousse for breakfast, lunch, and dinner for an entire week."

"Your mother let you eat twenty-one cups of mousse?" Ma said, staring down her long, thin nose. I held my breath, wishing I'd told her Geneva's mother was dead.

Geneva just grinned. "You mean Claudia? She ate it, too. She was celebrating her honeymoon. My father says she still eats like a kid. After all, she's only twenty-nine."

My father actually began coughing. My mother just

looked confused. I felt the same way. "Claudia—I mean, your stepmother—is only twenty-nine?" I repeated dumbly.

"How nice. It must be like having an older sister," Ma said in the kind of artificially sweetened voice people use to talk to infants and small dogs. I wished she'd just be quiet.

"Actually, Claudia is more like a younger sister," Geneva told her.

Ma gave her a sidelong glance. "Is that so?"

"Mmm-hmm. She doesn't cook, clean, or do the laundry. I'm constantly picking up her clothes from the floor. I iron Dad's shirts, and after school I do the grocery shopping. On the weekends, Claudia makes my father take her away because she thinks staying home is boring."

I couldn't help thinking of the oversize dust balls I'd seen when I visited. No wonder her house was so messy.

"Do you go along on the weekends?" Ma asked.

I felt like crawling under the table. I was used to having her conduct exhaustive investigations of my life, but doing it to my friends was going too far. "Ma . . . stop already!"

Geneva shook her head, making the bells in her ears tinkle. "Not very often. They offer to take me, but I usually have homework and studying to do. Most of the trips I told you about were when I was younger . . . before Dad married Claudia."

To my amazement, Ma nodded at Geneva approvingly. "You certainly seem to be a responsible young lady."

"We'd better have dessert now, Ma. We have to leave

for services soon," I said. I wanted to get out of the house before she could change her mind.

"Andi, did you tell your parents about the trip to Heavenly Vittles?" Geneva asked, as if on cue.

"Oh! I almost forgot about it." I took a piece of bread and began to butter it casually, trying to match her coolness. "Rabbi Jeff is organizing a group of kids to go down to the city Thanksgiving morning and help with the holiday meals at a soup kitchen. Can I go?"

"Well, those people are undernourished. They probably have a lot of diseases," Ma began.

"Exactly!" I agreed quickly. "That's why the Thanksgiving program is so important. It's the only meal a lot of people will get that day." I was still buttering my bread, but I noticed Ma had her eyes closed while I spoke.

"A lot of them have no place to bathe. They could have lice," she continued as if she hadn't heard a thing I'd said. "Andi, dear, isn't that an awful lot of butter you're using?"

People might be starving on Thanksgiving, and my mother was worried about my cholesterol level! "Ma, for once can't you think about—"

"Lower your voice," my father warned.

"We'd be back in plenty of time for dinner, Mrs. Applebaum," Geneva said politely. "And Rabbi Jeff will let us pick our own jobs at the soup kitchen. Andi and I were just planning to work in the back making Jell-O and stuff."

Ma smiled stiffly at her. "That kind of neighborhood is not safe for young girls."

"But we'll be driven right up to the door, Ma. We'll be in a group."

"All of those drugs down there . . . some of those people might be violent." Ma stood up and began clearing the serving platters, as if the discussion was finished.

Tears of frustration burned in the corners of my eyes. I bowed my head over my soup bowl to hide them and watched the ends of my hair float in the cream of mushroom.

"Rabbi Jeff says we'd be doing a mitzvah," Geneva said. *Mitzvah* is the Hebrew word for a deed that fulfills a commandment, a deed that will bring you God's blessing.

"Did he?" Ma was scraping the leftovers off our plates. I was painfully aware that there were enough of them to make a small mountain.

"Yes. He says volunteering at Heavenly Vittles is blessed work." Geneva stared modestly at her lap.

I didn't remember his putting it that way, but I don't think he would have minded, especially if he knew it would help persuade my mother. I sneaked a peek at Ma. She'd stopped stacking plates.

"Rabbi Jeff even said he's going to ask Rabbi Mandel to honor us at a Friday night service," Geneva added as if she'd just remembered.

I *knew* he'd never said anything like that. I shot her a questioning look, but she just gazed back at me innocently.

Ma lifted an armful of dishes and sighed loudly. "Well, if you stayed in the kitchen, it might be safe. What do you think, Howard?"

My father just nodded. He always agreed with my mother when there was a decision to be made about Mitchell or me. Maybe a long time ago he used to have his own convictions about raising us, but if so, he'd been no match for Ma.

"Okay, do your mitzvah," my mother said finally. "Just make sure you two stick together. It's safer that way."

9

Hillside's little sanctuary was nearly filled by the time my father dropped us off, and the only two empty seats together that we could find were in the first row. Geneva slid into hers casually and shrugged. "Well, I guess we'll have to pay attention."

I turned around in my chair to survey the crowd. Since a youth service meant it was okay for babies to cry and children to run up and down the aisles, there were a lot of parents with little kids. It looked like most of my Hillside classmates were there, as well as a whole bunch of older people who usually avoided the "kids' nights." I guess everyone was curious about what the new rabbinic intern's service would be like. I could hardly imagine a Friday night at Hillside without Rabbi Mandel's kind eyes and grandfatherly lectures. His services had a comfortable sameness, even if they were a teensy bit dull sometimes. I began to worry about how the adults in the room would react to bouncy, excitable Rabbi Jeff.

But when he finally strode up the center aisle in his

snowy white prayer shawl, he didn't seem nervous about taking Rabbi Mandel's place. His face radiated joy. At the sight of his blond ponytail pulled tight at the nape of his neck, I felt a little thrill run down my spine. I looked over at Geneva. Her eyes were large and shiny.

"*Shabbat shalom!*" Rabbi Jeff said, giving the traditional Sabbath greeting. "I feel a lot of energy flowing here tonight. I think we're going to be able to channel it into a very special experience." He stopped for a moment and looked over the congregation. When his eyes came to rest on Geneva and me, he broke out into an even broader smile. "I'm going to ask Geneva Peace and Andi Applebaum to light our candles and say the blessing tonight."

I sat there dazed for a moment. Beside me, Geneva stretched and stood up slowly. Only her little closed-mouth smile let me know that she was pleased with this surprise. "Come on, Andi," she hissed when I didn't move. Reluctantly, I followed her up to the podium, where Rabbi Jeff was beaming reassuringly. I smiled back, but inside, my stomach was tumbling like a clothes dryer. Even in Knowledge Bowl, I had to psych myself up before each match. The sense of being unprepared always terrified me.

Rabbi Jeff handed Geneva a paper with the blessing written out, just in case she'd forgotten it. To me he offered a box of wooden matches. There was only one problem: I'd never lit a match before. I didn't smoke, I'd never been camping, and even at my own bat mitzvah, my mother had struck the match and handed it to me for the candle-lighting ceremony. In their shiny silver candlesticks, two long white tapers stood waiting. I turned the box on its side and scratched it gently with a matchstick. Nothing happened, not even a spark.

"Press harder," Geneva whispered unhelpfully.

"I'm trying." I struck again, and this time a few sparks flew. I was so surprised, I dropped the match on the floor.

Geneva picked it up quickly and took the box from my hand. "Here, I'll do it. You read." She held out the page with the blessing. I could feel my face flaming bright as a candle.

"*Baruch atah, Adonai Eloheinu, melech haolam, asher kideshanu bemitsvotav, vetsivanu, lehadlik, ner shel Shabbat.* Blessed is Adonai, our God, who rules the universe and commands us to kindle the Sabbath lights."

I hadn't even noticed Rabbi Jeff come up behind us, but when I'd finished chanting, he laid a hand on my shoulder. "I guess I should tell you about the trick matches now," he said loud enough for everyone in the sanctuary to hear. "Of course, I slipped Geneva a real one earlier."

The congregation laughed as if he'd said something really funny, and I laughed along with them. In a split second, he'd saved me from looking like a total moron. Gratitude filled me up like a hot bowl of Ma's soup.

"You know, the year I worked with Save the Children in El Salvador, I helped plan an American-style party for the village mayor's eightieth birthday," Rabbi Jeff told the congregation while Geneva and I were still standing beside him. "It was a tiny hamlet in the mountains, so I wrote to my brother to send me some party stuff, like hats, blowers . . . and trick birthday candles. On the day of the party, my co-workers and I baked a big cake and stuck four boxes of candles in it. Then we lit them and set the whole thing down in front of the mayor. The entire population of the village was there. We got the mayor to make a wish and blow out the candles. The villagers gave him a thunderous round of applause." Rabbi Jeff paused, looking both mischievous and pleased with himself. "Suddenly, the candles relit themselves. The crowd gasped, the old man blew them out again, there was more applause . . . and the candles relit themselves again."

Everyone in the sanctuary was under Rabbi Jeff's spell. Even the babies had quieted down as if they could understand. Not only was he young, handsome, and funny, he was a truly caring human being. He'd been to El Salvador!

"Suddenly one of the villagers shouted, *Milagro!* which means 'miracle,' " Rabbi Jeff went on. "Right away, others took up the cry. I tried to explain that it was just a joke, but then I realized they weren't talking about the candles at all. They were celebrating the miracle of their mayor's life. The guy was eighty years old, and he'd been mayor for thirty years—and they loved him! Such abiding loyalty in the midst of a country torn to pieces by instability! Together those people and their mayor created their own miracle! It was the first time I understood that ordinary people could make miracles happen."

While the congregation murmured with pleasure,

Rabbi Jeff gave Geneva and me each a hug and sent us back to our seats. I took a furtive glance at the box of matches resting on the table next to the candles. They were the same ordinary brand my mother kept at home "for emergencies." Maybe he'd used trick candles in El Salvador, but to protect my ego tonight, he'd performed a different sort of trick.

For as long as I could remember, we'd recited the same prayer at every youth service. It was actually a poem written by an Israeli boy when he was thirteen. I opened my prayer book to the usual pages, but I saw the words as if they were new:

> I had a paint box—
> Each color glowing with delight;
> I had a paint box with colors
> Warm and cool and bright.
> I had no red for wounds and blood,
> I had no black for an orphaned child,
> I had no white for the face of the dead,
> I had no yellow for burning sands.
> I had orange for joy and life,
> I had green for buds and blooms,
> I had blue for clear bright skies,
> I had rose for dreams and rest.
> I sat down
> and painted
> Peace.

When we finished, Rabbi Jeff reached behind the podium and brought out a guitar. As he bent down, I noticed he was wearing a yarmulke with music notes crocheted around the rim. He began strumming while he spoke. "I'd like you to join me in singing about the joys of peace tonight. If you don't know the words, just hum along. The chorus is easy to learn."

His clear voice filled the sanctuary, and at the chorus, it was joined by the sweet voices of small children. In the night window, the reflection of the candles twinkled like new stars. I felt as snug as if I were in my own bed on a Saturday morning; only here, I was covered by a warm quilt of amber light, soft prayers, and familiar faces.

Beside me I could hear Geneva singing, and I joined her.

> *Peace is the bread we break*
> *Love is the river rolling*
> *Life is the chance we take*
> *When we make this earth our home!*

At the end of the service, it is traditional to give the person next to you a kiss. Geneva gave me a little hug as well. "The world is good tonight," she whispered. I squeezed her back.

Rabbi Jeff broke the spell with an announcement. "I'd like to extend our time together tonight with some danc-ing. I've brought along a tape of folk songs recorded by a group of friends. Let's just fold up all these chairs and stack them at the back to make room. The dances are easy to learn. Please stay."

Some people are natural dancers, but I'm not one of them. Just the mention of folk dancing made me nervous. Geneva, on the other hand, practically boogied those folding chairs off the floor. She couldn't wait to get started.

The music coming from the tape recorder combined several stringed instruments, flutes, a bongo drum, and a tambourine. It made me think of ancient celebrations on sandy shores, where biblical rivers flowed like honey. Yet the pepped up way R.J.'s friends sang gave it a kind of modern side, too. Looking like a cross between the Pied Piper and a rock star, Rabbi Jeff rounded up a bunch of little kids and marched them into the center of the sanctuary. Together they formed a circle and pranced around while the rest of us stood and watched. Then suddenly R.J. whirled out of the circle toward Geneva and me.

My heart began beating wildly as he approached. He was smiling a heart-stopping grin, and although I was terrified of tripping and stumbling over his feet, I couldn't resist smiling back. But he walked right by me and held out his hand for Geneva. She didn't hesitate a minute.

Geneva and Rabbi Jeff danced inside the circle of children, looking like a prince and princess from a fairy tale. I was nearly hypnotized by the way they whirled around, each turn faster and faster, her black hair flying out behind her and his golden ponytail whipping by. In the yellow glow of the candlelight, it seemed possible that a jealous sorceress might suddenly appear and freeze them in place for a hundred years.

When the next song began, Rabbi Jeff urged the rest of the congregation to join the circle, but he kept hold of Geneva's hand. I turned to go to the ladies' room, where I could be alone for a few minutes, and ran smack into Matt Gruenwald.

"Hey, I was just coming to show you something."

"What?" I hoped he'd think the redness in my face was just from the heat in the room.

Matt smiled evasively. "You've got to come outside to see."

I'd known Matt since I'd started going to Hillside. Up till now, the only mystery about him had been how he managed to grow from a short, skinny nuisance into a tall, skinny nuisance in a single year. I decided anything would be better than watching the prince and princess. "Let me get my jacket. I'll meet you out front."

The night air was cool and sharp. I found Matt, beaky nose aimed skyward, staring at the stars. "Okay, what are we out here for?"

He grinned and reached into his pocket. "I'm going to teach you to light a match." He produced the matchbox I'd left next to the candles and slid it open. "Go ahead, take one."

A sound that was somewhere between a laugh and a sob escaped from my throat. "I guess I looked pretty dumb up there."

"Well, let's just say it was obvious you were never a Girl Scout." He picked up a piece of gravel from the driveway and lobbed it off into the trees. "You know, tonight was the first time I ever saw you screw up at something. Do you realize that in all these years of religious school I have never once heard you miss an answer?"

"Gee, thanks." I wondered if he actually thought he was making me feel better. "It's kind of cold out here. I think I'll go back inside."

He blocked the entrance and held out the box of matches again. "Not until you light one."

"Well, okay, but we might be here a long time."

Matt shrugged, watching my face. "So?"

I dropped the first two matches as soon as they produced sparks. But on the third try, a bright yellow flame appeared and I managed to hold on to the stick. "Tah-dah!" I took a bow and started to shake out the flame.

"Wait! Give that to me," Matt ordered, taking the match from my hand. "Now close your eyes and make a wish before you blow it out."

"It's not my birthday," I protested.

He ignored me. "I'm going to burn my fingers if you don't hurry up."

"Okay, okay." I closed my eyes and wished I'd learn to dance. Then I puckered up to blow. I may have been really smart about school stuff, but I was still pretty dumb about real life. Matt kissed me.

My eyes flew open. "What are you doing?"

"You mean you don't know?"

"Of course I know." Actually, although I was almost fourteen, I'd never been kissed by a boy before. My heart was pumping out Morse code messages faster than I could read them: *Go back inside! No, stay here! Smile! Kiss him back! Don't just stand there, say something!!!*

Matt tilted his head and looked at me uncertainly. He was no prince, but he made me feel special. When I smiled at him, he grinned back and leaned toward me again—just as my father's car pulled into the driveway. Even at temple, Dad always picked me up early.

"I've got to get Geneva," I told Matt before I turned and ran. My father was supposed to drive her home, since her father and Claudia were out somewhere.

When I got back inside, the dancing was over. Rabbi Jeff, Geneva, and a few adults were gathered in a corner of the room. Geneva was scribbling away as if she were taking notes.

"My dad's here," I whispered, coming up behind her. "We've got to go."

"Give me a few minutes. We're planning a canned-food drive for Heavenly Vittles," she said, not looking up from her notepad.

One of the cardinal rules in my family was "Never keep your parents waiting." If I did and we were late getting home, Ma would have plenty to say. "Geneva," I murmured in her ear, "we really have to leave now."

She continued to write as if she hadn't heard me. I tried to look interested while the little group continued their meeting. "I can probably get you a case of canned soup from my brother-in-law's store," one man offered.

R.J. clapped him on the shoulder. "That would be super!"

Geneva added *Soup—Mr. Felson* to her list. When she was finished, I nudged her gently. "Geneva, I think we'd better—"

"Shh!"

But time was ticking quickly by. Any minute, Dad

might come in looking for me, the way the parents of the preschoolers did. I positioned myself in front of her so she couldn't ignore me. *"Geneva, please."*

"Look, you go on out. I'll be there soon," she snapped. Her lower lip stuck out angrily.

"I can take you home, Geneva," Rabbi Jeff offered. "That way Andi won't have to wait."

Geneva beamed at him. "Great!"

"Well, I guess I'll see you," I mumbled, backing away. My cheeks were burning with embarrassment.

"Yeah, sure." Geneva didn't give me so much as a glance.

Only moments before, I couldn't wait to tell her about Matt. Now I knew I'd never mention it.

10

In the morning as I lay in bed, the memory of my first kiss came back to me. If I shut my eyes, I could still taste peppermint Chap Stick and cold air laced with the sulfur scent of burning matches. I pulled the quilt over my head and summoned up Matt's face. Bells began ringing. After a few moments, I realized it was the telephone.

"Hello?"

"Hi, Andi, what are you doing?" Geneva's voice was light and cheery.

Even though I was alone, I blushed. But my embarrassment was quickly followed by resentment when I remembered the way she'd acted last night. "Nothing much," I answered in as flat a voice as I could manage.

"Good, because you've got to come over. There's something important we need to do!"

I forced a yawn into the receiver. "Oh, really? What?"

"I can't say over the phone. I'll tell you when you get here."

"I'm busy today, Geneva. There's an essay for English

due on Monday, and I promised my friend I'd stop over at Lazy Hollow High to watch the Pom Girls work out." The truth was, I'd called Marci in the middle of the week to see if she might want to get together today, and she'd graciously agreed to let me view the Pom Girls in action. The rest of the weekend, she was "all tied up."

"What's the matter with you?" Geneva burst out. "This is important!"

"Well, maybe I had something important to tell you last night," I countered. It was hard to keep from letting her know just how mad I really was.

"Did you?" she asked after a pause. "I'm really sorry. Sometimes I just can't help getting involved. Anyway, you can tell me everything when you get here. We've got all day."

She sounded sincere. Probably she hadn't realized how rude she'd been. But I hadn't seen Marci even once since school started, and I wanted to drop by the Pom Girls for a visit, at least for a little while. I remembered that Marci had said her practice started at eleven. "I'll see if I can get my dad to drop me off at your house around twelve," I told Geneva.

"Perfect! My father and Claudia will be gone by then."

"Okay. See you later then." I wondered why she didn't want her father or stepmother around, and whether or not I'd ever get to meet them.

After I hung up, I dialed Marci's number. "Hi, Marce, it's Andi," I said when she answered. "I'll only be able to stay for about an hour of Pom Girls practice this morning. I hope that's okay."

There was dead silence on the other end. Then Marci began stuttering, "Gee, I . . . don't worry about it . . . I mean, today's practice is canceled."

"When did you find out?" I could feel the blood rushing to my face in quick, angry pulses.

"Yesterday. Look, I was just going to call you. Maybe we can meet in the Village later. I'm going to be down there with Sharon and a few other people."

I had to swallow a thick lump in my throat before I could speak. "Sorry, I'll be busy all afternoon."

"Maybe you can come to next week's practice."

"Yeah, maybe." I hung up the receiver. Then I whispered good-bye to my best friend.

• • •

Geneva practically pulled me through the door the moment I rang the bell. "Guess what? I found his address in the phone book!"

"Whose?" I asked as she draped an arm over my shoulder and propelled me into the kitchen. I was overwhelmed by her gesture. She seemed so glad to have me around.

"Rabbi Jeff's! Now we can see where he lives." She poured herself a cup of coffee. "Want some?"

I shook my head no; I still drank milk. "You mean go over there?"

"Of course!" Geneva seemed surprised that I wasn't following her thinking. She sprang up onto the kitchen counter and sat with her long legs dangling over the side. "We don't have to go inside or anything. We'll just hang out and maybe run into him."

"Why?"

"Because he's hot!"

I wished she wouldn't call him that. I mean, he was a religious leader in training and all. But I knew if I protested, Geneva would think I was a wimp. "That's not a reason to spy on him," I said, trying logic.

"It's not spying, it's . . . doing research." She smiled as if she were pleased she'd come up with a respectable alternative.

"You do research on famous people like George Washington and Madame Curie, Geneva. You don't do it on your Hebrew teachers."

The little lips-closed smile appeared on her face. "You do when you're in love."

I pulled out a chair from the round white table and sat. True, Geneva was mature for her age, but did she really think she had a chance with a guy in his twenties—a rabbi yet? Someone older than Mitchell? Then I remembered that her father had married a woman at least ten years younger. Maybe the age difference didn't seem that unusual to her.

"Come with me, Andi. I need moral support."

Well, what harm could it do? We could watch his door the way I'd seen it done in detective movies. Maybe we'd get to see his friends, or even a girlfriend. That should bring Geneva back to reality. And if R.J. himself actually appeared, we could duck behind a tree. "Okay, why not?" I agreed.

"Great! I knew I could depend on you." She jumped down off the counter, put her coffee cup in the sink, and grabbed her father's car keys off the hook on the wall. "Let's go."

"Couldn't we walk?" I asked weakly. "Or take a bus?"

"Sure, if you've got all weekend. He lives in Highbank."

I'd been to the mall in Highbank with my mother plenty of times. The town was a lot bigger than either Reed or Lazy Hollow, and the streets were full of traffic. It was a serious place. "I don't know, Geneva. Last time we only drove around here. We'd have to take some major roads. Highbank's miles away."

She turned her back to me and ran the water in the sink full force. Furiously, she began sloshing it in her abandoned cup. "I thought you said I was a good driver. Don't you trust me?"

I didn't know what to say. The question reminded me of a time in third grade when two sixth graders had cornered me in the playground and demanded my snack money. They claimed they were starting a bank for us younger kids because we were always losing our change while playing games like jump rope and tag. "Don't you trust us?" the taller one, a chunky redhead, had asked when I hesitated. If I said yes, I knew the money was gone forever. If I said no, I'd receive a punch, and they'd get my money anyhow. Either way, I lost.

"Well, yeah, I trust you, but something could happen. Without it being your fault, I mean. What if we get lost . . . or we're hit by another car . . . or stopped by the police . . . or have a breakdown?"

Geneva seemed to regain her composure. She shut off

the water and turned to me, eyes wide with concern. "Andi, Andi, you've got to stop worrying about every little thing. You're starting to sound exactly like your mother."

• • •

The good thing about driving and talking is, you don't have to look at the person you're with. It's a lot like talking on the phone. You're just a disembodied voice, without facial expressions or body language. It makes it easier to talk about serious things.

"So what did you want to tell me last night?" Geneva asked once we were on the road.

My hand squeezed the door handle. "It wasn't really that important."

"Let me guess. . . . It had something to do with your brother, right? Your mother seemed pretty weird about him at dinner. Is he sick or something?"

"Yeah, he's sick all right. He's sick of my parents." I was surprised at the force of my answer.

"What do you mean?"

"Just that I haven't seen Mitchell since June. He was supposed to come home for Rosh Hashanah, but he backed out because he and my parents are always fighting. He thinks they're trying to run his life. Ma and Dad even threatened not to pay his school tuition next year if he doesn't start showing up more often, but Mitch got a job pumping gas, so he'll be able to pay his own way."

"Do you miss him?"

I looked out the window at houses that all looked the same, right down to the swing sets each father had put together in the tiny side yards. A long time ago, my brother and I had played on one just like them. Mitchell, six years older than me, had always been the leader—the chief Ghostbuster. We'd laughed about those games the last time we'd talked. It was just before school started, and I'd admitted I was nervous about starting Barf.

"Don't worry, all schools are alike, except maybe at Barth they'll have Champagne Bowl instead of Knowledge Bowl," Mitch had said. "If anyone gives you a hard time, just slime 'em."

In spite of my nerves, I'd laughed. "Remember when we used Dad's shaving cream to play *Ghostbusters?* We dripped green food coloring down the spout to make slime, and when we were finished, we just put the can back in the bathroom."

"Dad's face had a green tint for an entire week!" Mitch had crowed. "Or maybe that was Ma's cooking."

At the mention of our mother, we both fell silent for a few seconds. "Mitch, are you going to come home soon?"

"Well, sure," he had answered, so quickly I thought he must be lying. "I wouldn't miss Rabbi Mandel's New Year's sermon."

"Really?"

"Of course. Besides, the Mets play the Dodgers that weekend. Don't you want to go?"

"Yeah!" I had totally believed him, and I'd looked forward to going for weeks. Now I wasn't sure whether I was madder at him for lying or at myself for being so gullible.

"Earth to Andi, do you read me?" Geneva's voice drew me back to the present.

"Sorry, I guess I was daydreaming," I said thickly.

She stared at the road ahead. "Listen, after a while it gets easier."

I knew she was thinking about her mother, who would never be home again. I nodded and turned back to the window. We rode on for a few minutes without talking. It was kind of peaceful, as if the car were a big cradle rocking the blues away.

"Maybe we can visit your brother sometime," Geneva said, breaking the silence.

I didn't know if she meant we should take the train or if she was actually thinking of driving to Philadelphia, but all I said was "Maybe."

• • •

We found Rabbi Jeff's street easily. It was right off the main road, just a few blocks from the Highbank Mall. Geneva pulled up alongside the curb directly across the street from number thirty-seven, which according to the phone book was his address. It was part of a row of attached houses that were painted alternately yellow and brown. Number thirty-seven was brown.

"Now what?" I asked when she'd shut off the engine.

She propped her chin on the steering wheel. "We wait until he comes out."

"We don't even know if he's home," I reminded her. "All his shades are pulled down. Ma does that whenever she leaves the house."

But in less than ten minutes, the door opened and

Rabbi Jeff stepped outside, looking like a regular person in his jean jacket and sneakers. "Get down!" I squealed, as he bounded down the front steps. I slid under the seat so quickly that I bumped my head on the dashboard. My heart was pounding.

But instead of slinking behind the wheel, Geneva flipped the door handle and leaped out of the car. "Come on!" she shouted over her shoulder.

I couldn't believe she was going to follow him! What if he turned around and caught her? How would she explain being here? My mouth was dry as I lifted my head and peered through the windshield. Geneva was actually chasing him.

There was no sense being left behind. I couldn't get home without her, anyway. I jumped out of the car and ran across the street as Geneva began to call, "R.J.! Jeffrey!" My stomach lurched miserably.

He whirled around just as I caught up to Geneva. For an instant I thought he might not recognize us. Then he broke into a broad grin. "Geneva! Andi! What are you two doing here?"

"We're on our way to the mall. Andi's father dropped us off," Geneva said easily.

"On this street?"

"Dad had a home-decorating consultation in the neighborhood," I said. I felt unnerved at how effortlessly I could lie.

"Great! We can walk together. I'm going to see a friend who lives near the mall."

We started out three abreast on the sidewalk, with

Geneva in the center. Actually, I had to jog to keep up. After a block, I gave in and fell back a step. They didn't seem to notice.

"You know, I'm glad we ran into each other," R.J. told Geneva. "I've been thinking about last night."

"I could hardly even sleep," she murmured.

He nodded. "Yeah. I think we share the same feelings."

"We do!" Geneva exclaimed.

"What I mean is, every human being has basic needs that must be met. . . ."

I couldn't believe my ears! Less than three minutes had passed, and the conversation was already reminding me of the romance rack of our local bookstore. I felt like I should give them some privacy, but at the same time, I didn't want to miss anything.

Rabbi Jeff touched her arm. "That's why this food and fund-raising drive is so important. We've got to help Heavenly Vittles build its stockpile, so it can provide for even more members of the community. I'm asking some people to come to Hillside next Tuesday night to start packing the clothes and food donations. Can you make it?"

"Ohh!" I said, before I could shut my mouth.

The two of them looked at me. "You too, Andi," Rabbi Jeff added, as if he suddenly remembered I was there. He turned back to Geneva. "I know I can count on your help."

She squeezed his arm back and stared up into his eyes. "Yes, yes, count on me."

At the next corner, R.J. slowed his walk and waved

vaguely toward the right. "Well, here's where I turn off. See you Tuesday!"

We stood and watched as he walked halfway up the street and disappeared into an apartment building. Geneva hugged her sides and said dreamily, "Did you hear what he said? He's been thinking about me."

"Actually, he said he was thinking about *last night*," I corrected her. "I think he meant the food drive."

"Andi, sometimes you are so naive!" she exclaimed, shaking her head in disbelief. "You've got to learn to read between the lines. I mean, he couldn't just come out and say what he feels. Not now, anyway. After all, he's almost a rabbi."

She hadn't seemed to think that mattered before, but I didn't challenge her. I was still depending on her to drive me back. And besides, there was a slight chance she might be right, wasn't there? After all, when Mitchell was home, I'd seen him act pretty weird around girls. The more he liked them, the more he'd tease. He had this one girlfriend, Thea, who used to come over on Fridays, which was the day my mother spent at the store with my dad. Thea and Mitchell would always start out in the kitchen. They'd make popcorn, and he'd throw some at her. To get him back, she'd blow soda at him through a straw. Then he'd chase her around the kitchen with an ice cube, and when he caught her . . . well, they always ended up kissing. It was pretty confusing.

11

*O*ur first stop at the mall was a lingerie shop filled with lacy underwear and the skimpiest nighties imaginable. Just looking in the window made me self-conscious, but Geneva marched right in and pulled two slinky white gowns off a rack. "Claudia has one just like this," she told me. "Come on, let's see how they look."

I followed her to the dressing room feeling so giddy I was afraid I might burst out laughing. Any minute I expected to be stopped by a disapproving sales clerk. With my mother, shopping trips always had a specific purpose—shoes or jeans or whatever. Ma acted like shopping was a job: find what you need, pay, and leave. With Marci, it had been more leisurely. We'd wandered in and out of shops at the mini-mall near home, but we'd only tried on things we might actually buy, never stuff like this.

The negligee looked terrific on Geneva, who had a real chest and shapely legs instead of two strands of spaghetti like mine. Looking in the mirror was totally depressing. No wonder gorgeous R.J. was interested in Geneva and noodle-necked Matt was chasing me.

We left the dressing room and went off to have a banana split for lunch. Afterward, I bought a peppermint Chap Stick and Geneva got a bumper sticker that said Hunger Isn't a Crime—It's a Shame. Then we headed back to the car.

I was a little worried that we might run into R.J. again—what if he saw Geneva get behind the wheel?—but to my relief, he didn't reappear. As we pulled away, I looked at my watch; it was three o'clock. Dad was picking me up at Geneva's at four. We still had plenty of time.

Geneva was in a great mood. While she drove, we sang old Beatles songs—"Hey Jude" and "Strawberry Fields Forever"—at the top of our lungs. It seemed like only a few minutes had passed before Highbank disappeared. I recognized the little houses with the matching swing sets just as the car began slowing down.

"What's the matter, did you see a cop?" I asked.

"No. I don't know. The car won't go any faster." She pressed her foot down on the gas pedal, but we hardly moved.

I leaned over and looked at the gas gauge. A sinking feeling came over me. "Geneva, look. We're out of gas!"

"Then I guess I'll just stop here." She made it sound like a joke. We rolled to the curb and bumped to a stop.

"Now what?" I had to fight back tears. The thought of having to ask my parents to rescue us was terrifying. I tried to think of someone else we could call. Mitchell was hundreds of miles away, too far to be of any use. And if we called R.J. for help, he'd probably tell our parents anyway. While we sat there, a policeman in a patrol car passed by. What if he returned? I couldn't help sniffling.

Geneva had been rummaging through the glove compartment. She turned to me with a cigarette dangling from her lips and lit it as I watched. "Come on, Andi, don't worry." She blew out a stream of smoke. "I just remembered my dad keeps a gas can in the trunk."

We got out and walked around to the back. As soon as she raised the trunk lid, I saw the red can. Relief made my knees wobbly.

Geneva hoisted the can out of the car. "Which way do you think we ought to go?"

"What do you mean?"

She shook the can. "It's empty. We've got to find a gas station to fill it up."

"Oh." I looked up and down the busy street, wide enough for two lanes of traffic in each direction. All I could see were houses and trees. "I guess we should walk back toward Highbank," I ventured. "That's where most of the cars are headed."

"Good thinking." She threw down her cigarette and crushed it with the heel of her boot.

We trudged along the side of the road, stopping at each corner to peer down the side streets. Occasionally, Geneva would say something, but I was too nervous to give much of an answer. "There!" I shouted when I spotted a station about a quarter mile ahead of us. We'd walked eleven blocks, and all the while I'd been conscious of my watch ticking away the time that was left before my father showed up at Geneva's.

I grabbed the can from her, ready to run the rest of the way. "Wait a minute," she said, putting a hand on my arm. "How much money have you got left?"

I thrust my hand down into my jacket pocket and found a dollar and four cents. "What about you?" I asked.

She pulled some change out of her jeans. "All I've got is ninety-five cents."

"Is it enough?"

She ran a hand through her hair. "Well, gas costs at least a dollar twenty a gallon. All we can afford is one."

It was no use. Obviously I deserved this for lying to a rabbi and driving around with Geneva. Now that I was a juvenile delinquent, I understood that old saying "Crime doesn't pay." I closed my eyes before I spoke. "Will that be enough to get us home?"

"Yeah, I guess."

"Then come on!" I started toward the station again.

I waited while the attendant screwed the gas cap back on a blue van and took the driver's money. "Hi. Could you put one gallon in here?" I asked, trying to sound natural.

He looked at the can without making a move to take it. "One? That thing holds five." He was heavy and grimy and badly in need of a shave. I couldn't tell whether he was twenty-five or thirty-five. A ragged cigarette hung in the corner of his mouth. It gave him sort of a permanent sneer.

"All we need is a gallon," Geneva said beside me. The attendant's lazy gaze wandered over to her. The way he stared gave me the creeps. Geneva must have felt the same way. She pulled her jacket closed.

"What for? Neither of you's old enough to drive." The attendant made it sound like a challenge. Somewhere in Pennsylvania, my brother was probably filling up a tank right now. I wondered whether I could figure out how to operate a pump myself.

"My mother ran out of gas," I squeaked nervously. "She's waiting for us in the car."

The attendant's eyes were still fixed on Geneva. "Where's the car at?"

"Just a few blocks back there. Not far," she told him. I could tell from her voice that she was uneasy.

I held out the can. "Could you hurry up? I don't want my mother to worry."

He ran his blackened fingertips through his hair. An image of his pillowcase, bad-smelling and soiled with dark oily smudges, made my stomach contract. He winked or squinted at Geneva. "Your little sister's got a big mouth."

A change seemed to come over Geneva. She flashed him a wide, friendly smile. "Yeah. Cool it, Andi." She took the gas can from me and held it out to him. He leaned up very close to her as he accepted it.

In spite of my fear, I felt insulted at being taken for Geneva's pesty little sister. But as soon as the attendant's back was turned, she whispered, "Sorry. I had to say that. You'd better give me your money now . . . and shut up till we're out of here." I handed it over. She pulled her change out as well. When he came back with the can, she pushed the change and the crumpled bill into his hand. "Here."

He examined the money. "There's an extra eighty cents here."

"That's okay, keep it." She smiled brightly and reached for the can, but he held it back.

"How 'bout I drive you to your car? It ain't busy here anyway."

I followed his gaze to where a black pickup truck was parked. It had the kind of windows that were tinted dark, so you couldn't see inside. Anything could happen to you behind those windows and no one would know. My heart began to thrash against my ribs. I thought of screaming at Geneva to run, but I wasn't sure whether I was overreacting. Silently, I promised God that if we got home alive today, I'd never get in the car with Geneva again.

"Nah, that's okay. Our mother would kill us for accepting a ride with a stranger. We've got to go. She's probably flagging down a police car right now." Geneva reached over and put a hand on the gas can, and the attendant released it.

"Come on, Andi," she said, although I was right beside her. She grabbed my hand, and we started walking very quickly.

Out of the corner of my eye, I saw the attendant take two steps after us, then stop. "You girls come back soon." He laughed as if he thought something was funny.

Geneva and I half walked and half ran back to the

car, still holding hands. We were breathing too hard even to talk. By the time we got there, little pearls of perspiration were glistening off the tops of her eyebrows. I collapsed against the side of the car while she poured the gas into the tank.

"That was so scary!" I gasped. "I thought we were going to end up on the front page of tomorrow's newspaper."

"I know. I would've run out of there, except that he had our gas can." She shook the last few drops into the tank and screwed the cap back on. Then she swung around to face me. "Did you see his truck? It was darker than a hearse!" She giggled nervously.

"Yeah! One ride and you turn into bride of Dracula!" I began to laugh, but at the same time, I checked the road behind us to make sure there was no black pickup approaching.

Geneva looked at her watch. "Hey, we'd better get going. We don't want to keep your father waiting." She plunked the can into the trunk and shut it with a thud. "One thing's for sure. Before we take our next drive, we check the gas gauge first."

12

Ma donated a dozen cans of tuna to the Heavenly Vittles drive and an old pair of warm gloves she unearthed from the basement. Dad threw in two thick flannel shirts he hadn't really worn much and six yellow-striped throw pillows that someone had ordered but never picked up. "Everyone likes pillows," he assured me, packing each one individually in a plastic bag. I had a ridiculous vision of people stretched out on park benches with yellow-striped pillows under their heads, but I took them anyway.

At the back of my closet, I discovered a ski jacket that I'd outgrown and a smallish purple sweater I'd hesitated to give away before. I tossed them both in a bag and went into Mitchell's room, where I found the frayed navy pullover he'd loved to wear senior year. I pressed the sleeve to my face for a moment, then added it to my collection. Mitch would want to contribute something, too.

On Tuesday night I dragged the load to Hillside. A

lot of my classmates were already there, sorting through the bags that other families had dropped off. Geneva was sitting at the head of a long table, making notes on a yellow pad. She was so absorbed, she didn't even see me approaching. I looked over her shoulder at a list of clothing, carefully divided into type and size.

"Hi!" I said, surprising her. "Believe it or not, my folks actually gave me a ton of stuff to bring. Want some help?"

She looked up and smiled at something behind me. "Um, I think we need someone to work on the food."

I turned around. R.J. was on his way into the room, carrying a teetering stack of cardboard boxes. He returned her smile before he noticed me. "Andi! I have a job for you."

"Okay." I helped him set the boxes down in a corner. "What should I do?"

"I'd like you to organize the food. You'll need someone to help you." He surveyed the group. "Matt, can you give Andi a hand over here?"

"Sure!" Matt was on his knees, unpacking clothes with Jordan and Samantha. In an instant, he bounded up on his spidery legs and joined us. When he stood next to our rabbinic intern, I realized they were about the same height. For some weird reason that made me smile.

"First we need to sort," R.J. told us, nodding toward a pile of grocery bags. "Maybe the two of you can unpack some of these bundles and put the stuff in groups, like fruit, protein, snacks. Use your own judgment. Afterward, you can make up a list of what we've got."

"Taking inventory is my specialty," I assured him. Ever since I was a little kid, I'd helped my father take inventory in his store, only instead of food, I'd counted cans of paint, brushes, window shades, shower curtains, and stuff.

R.J. winked at Matt. "Then I leave you in good hands." He walked off toward Geneva again.

"Light any fires lately?" Matt teased when our leader was gone.

I don't know what came over me. "No, I'm into other crimes these days," I murmured.

Matt looked at me skeptically. "What do you do, litter?"

I hadn't breathed a word to anyone about my trips with Geneva. Not to Mitchell, who hadn't phoned lately anyway, or to Marci, whom I hadn't spoken to since she'd neglected to tell me about the canceled Pom Girls practice. The only one who knew my secret was my Barf classmate Alana, and she never let me forget it. She sat in front of me in algebra, and whenever she turned around to copy the answers to the homework (which was practically every day), she asked, "So you want to go to Yum Yum's for ice cream later?"

"I don't do that anymore," I whispered, which just made her laugh.

"Don't be silly. Everyone eats ice cream."

Even though I knew it was the wimp's way out, I let her see my homework. I thought of it as insurance, although some people might call it blackmail.

But here with Matt in Hillside's familiar sanctuary it was different. I *wanted* him to know. "I drive," I said quietly.

"What?"

"I drive cars, or sometimes I just ride in them and let Geneva drive."

He still looked as if he didn't understand. "You've got to be kidding."

"I'm not." My heart began racing, but I had to continue. "We've been to Yum Yum's and over to Highbank." I decided not to mention R.J.

Creases appeared across his forehead, and his mouth became a thin, straight line. "Do you steal cars, too?"

"No, of course not! Geneva borrows her family's car when they're not home." It hadn't occurred to me that using the Peaces' car could be considered stealing, but now I experienced a weakness behind my knees.

Matt looked over to where Geneva and R.J. were packing piles of sweaters in cartons. "Well, it must be her fault. She's always seemed a little cracked."

"She is not!" I hissed. "You don't know anything about her. She's just more freethinking than all the little minds around here, including you. Just forget I ever mentioned it." Obviously, telling him anything had been a big, fat mistake. I knelt down and began unloading a brown paper bag.

Matt dropped down next to me and pulled at the carpet. "Calm down. I'm sorry! I admit I don't know her. But driving without a license in a borrowed car could get you in a lot of trouble. I mean, I wouldn't ever tell, but you could get caught. I'm just . . . worried about you."

"I'm not going to do it anymore anyway," I said, as much to myself as to him. I had nightmares about my last drive with Geneva. Every time I saw a black pickup with tinted windows, I felt positively ill. I looked him in the eye. "I really mean it."

"Good." He tilted his head and looked at me the way he had after his surprise kiss. In spite of my anger a moment before, my lips got all tingly. "Why'd you tell me, anyway?" he asked in a soft voice.

A rush of warm feeling filled me up, and I punched him lightly on the arm. "I think you and I are going to be friends."

We got to work unpacking the bags. The most popular items were peanut butter, applesauce, canned spaghetti, and tuna, followed by pineapple rings, peas and carrots, chicken noodle soup, and tomato juice. Matt unloaded the last bag, which held eight cans of artichoke hearts, four jars of black olives, and a half dozen cans of sardines.

"Someone sure has weird tastes," he joked, clutching his throat as he stacked up the sardines.

I started to giggle. "I hear if you mix this stuff together, it makes a great salad."

"Yeah, right." Matt grabbed his middle and rolled on the floor dramatically, which only made me laugh harder.

"What's so funny?" Geneva asked, suddenly looming above us.

"Just someone's idea of nutrition," Matt answered before I could stop him. He held up the olives. "These must be really filling—the can says they're *giant* olives." I had to stifle a smile.

"A lot you know," Geneva snapped haughtily. "Olives happen to be rich in iron." She looked Matt's body over appraisingly and sniffed. "You ought to try eating some."

"Ouch!" Matt murmured. "I didn't mean to—"

Geneva cut him off. "Andi, I just came to ask if you can have dinner with Dad, Claudia, and me on Friday. It's my birthday."

"Sure! I didn't know it was . . . ," I began, but Geneva had already turned on her heel and walked away.

13

*ff*ter school on Friday, I caught the bus to Reed. As I staggered up the aisle looking for a seat, I thought about Geneva's stepmother. Would she actually cook something, I wondered, or would we be having takeout? I could just imagine her on the telephone to the local Chinese restaurant, long red nails tapping the receiver as she ordered in a high, whiny voice.

From the rear of the bus, someone waved me out of my daydream: Alana Voegel-Whitcroft, my friendly blackmailer. My heart sank. I'd forgotten she lived in Reed, too. But it was too late to pretend I hadn't noticed her. When I got closer, she slid over so I could sit beside her.

"You didn't by any chance finish the math homework in school, did you?" she asked, before I could kick my book bag under the seat. Alana never beat around the bush. You had to admire that.

I extracted the homework from my notebook and handed it over, hoping for once I had all the wrong answers.

"Thanks. I'll give it back to you Monday morning." She tucked the paper inside her book and gave it a satisfied pat. "Where are you going, anyway?"

"To visit my friend."

Alana was examining her nails, which were polished and perfectly rounded. "The one who drove with you to Yum Yum's?"

"Her name is Geneva."

"Oh, right." I saw her eyes slip sideways to watch me. "So have you done much driving lately?"

"I told you I don't do that anymore."

"Yes, but what about your friend?" She licked her top lip and watched me closely. "Or maybe she's not as hot as she thinks she is?"

I knew what Alana was doing, but it didn't matter. All I could think of was the first day of school, when she and her friends had treated me like a loser. Geneva was cooler than Alana would ever be, and she was my friend. I couldn't keep my mouth shut. "She still drives . . . sometimes."

"Where do you go?" Alana kept on picking away like I was an old coat of nail polish. "I haven't seen you two around town."

"That's the point of driving. We don't hang out in Reed," I said, filling my voice with as much disdain as I could muster.

"Yeah, Reed's a drag," she agreed. "Where do you usually hang out?" Her pink tongue peeked out through her teeth, reminding me of my neighbor's Lhasa apso.

I told myself Geneva wouldn't mind my saying where

we'd been. "Different places . . . the Highbank Mall."
Alana's eyes shone with approval. I looked past her out
the window, wondering why I felt like I'd given away
something that wasn't mine. "Here's my stop," I said,
suddenly recognizing the familiar street. I gathered up
my stuff and turned to Alana. "I'll see you Monday."

"Wait, take this." She tore off a scrap of paper and
scribbled something.

I looked at the slip curiously. "Is this your phone
number?"

She gave a quick, embarrassed nod, followed by a little
shrug. "Maybe sometime we can all go for a ride
together."

"Yeah, sure."

• • •

Someone was unloading groceries from the Peaces' car
as I walked up the driveway. Her buttery blond ponytail
swung back and forth as she ducked in and out of the
trunk, setting bulging brown bags on the pavement. She
didn't notice me right away, and I stopped to listen to
what she was humming: the old Beatles song "Strawberry
Fields Forever," which Geneva sometimes sang. When
she turned around, I read her sweatshirt—Skytrain
Airlines—before I looked up into her wide blue eyes.

"You must be Andi," she said, as she rested a bag on
her hip. "I'm glad I'm finally getting to meet you. I'm
Claudia."

Geneva's stepmother practically looked young enough
to have been a friend of Mitchell's. But what really surprised me was that she'd been grocery shopping. Geneva

had led me to believe that Claudia never did anything motherly. Ever.

"Oh, hi." I could feel myself stiffen. It was impossible not to feel unfriendly toward the person who Geneva claimed had made her into a household slave.

"Could you take this?" Claudia asked, holding out a sack with long, feathery carrot tops dangling over the edge. As I took it from her, I saw it was also filled with plump, shiny tomatoes and green peppers as big as an ogre's ears.

Claudia picked up two other bags and headed for the front door. "I'm making Geneva's favorite tonight, lasagna primavera—that's with veggies. Of course you know she's a vegetarian."

I nodded uncomfortably and followed her. I clearly remembered Geneva telling Ma that Claudia didn't cook, but here I was carrying groceries for lasagna primavera. If it was Geneva's favorite dish, didn't that mean Claudia had made it before?

"Geneva, your friend's here!" Claudia shouted as she pushed inside.

Geneva padded midway down the staircase on her long, bare feet and hung lazily over the banister. It reminded me of the rude way she'd slouched against the counter at Yum Yum's when we'd met Alana. "Hi, Andi, c'mon up," she called, eyeing the brown bag I was carrying. She didn't say anything to Claudia, not even offering to help with the groceries for her birthday dinner.

"I'll be up in a sec," I said, heading for the kitchen, where Claudia had already disappeared. Geneva shrugged, but she came down the stairs and followed me.

I set the bag on the table while Claudia unloaded vegetables into the refrigerator. "You wouldn't believe what red peppers cost today," she announced. "That store manager should be arrested for price-gouging!"

Geneva rolled her eyes mockingly at Claudia's back. I tried to pretend I hadn't noticed.

"I got you a jar of olives stuffed with almonds. I thought you'd like them instead of pimentos for a change," Claudia continued breezily. "And they had those bread sticks that you like, the kind with the sesame seeds on them. They're in one of those bags if you want to snack on them now."

"No, thanks," Geneva said flatly. She didn't even ask if I wanted any. "C'mon, Andi, let's go upstairs."

I looked over at Claudia. "See you later," I murmured. Geneva shot me a dirty look.

We were headed for the stairs when the phone began ringing. "Gen, would you please pick up? My hands are full," Claudia called.

Geneva clicked her tongue against her teeth in annoyance. She spun around, fists clenched, and stalked back to the kitchen. But her face brightened when she put the receiver to her ear. "Oh, hi, Dad, what's up?" She glanced over at Claudia, who was scraping carrots at the sink. "Yeah, she's here. I'll put her on in a minute. What time are you coming home? Early, great! Andi's already here."

At the mention of my name, I smiled at Geneva, but her eyes narrowed into two glowing points. "My friend from Hillside!" she exclaimed sharply. "I told you last night she was coming for dinner, remember?" She sighed in exasperation and held out the phone to Claudia. "He wants to speak to you."

Claudia wiped her hands on her jeans and took the receiver. I thought we'd go up to Geneva's room, but she hung around to eavesdrop.

"Can't we make it another night, Jason? I was planning to make Geneva a special birthday dinner," Claudia said after listening a moment. She lowered her voice when she realized we were still there.

While Geneva's father spoke, Claudia wound the telephone cord around her wrist over and over again. After a few moments, she sighed and closed her eyes. "Maybe you could change the time . . . make it an hour later, so we could have a quick bite here first."

I sneaked a peek at Geneva. She was leaning in the doorway, head down, staring at the floor. With one hand, she swept her hair forward and fondled the wish braid at the back of her neck. I felt under my hair for mine. Up till now, I'd practically forgotten about it.

"Well, what about on the other end?" Claudia's voice had risen a bit. "Maybe we can come home early." Her eyes darted over Geneva's hunched frame. When Geneva raised her head, Claudia looked away. "Tomorrow? But . . . yes, yes, I see. All right, I'll be ready." She bit her lip as she hung up.

"I'm so sorry, Gen. Your father and I have to go out tonight. We're meeting the Burgesses, those people who own the travel agency Jason is thinking of acquiring.

They're leaving for Boca tomorrow; there's just no other time. Maybe Andi can come back tomorrow to celebrate. I feel really bad about this."

"Yeah, sure," Geneva sneered. "I know how important your meeting is." She turned to me. "Did I tell you Claudia was a stewardess when my father met her? After they were married, he got her to quit. Now he's going to buy her a travel agency to keep her busy."

Claudia looked stung. "Being nasty isn't going to change anything, Geneva. This is business. It has nothing to do with how your dad feels about you."

"Were you out for a business dinner last night, too?" Geneva's face was an angry knot. "Oh, no, I forgot. You were celebrating another anniversary. I believe it was your two hundredth day of married bliss, wasn't it?"

"That isn't fair, Geneva. You said you didn't want to come along." Claudia's voice was practically a whisper.

"Well, two's company, three's a crowd, isn't it?" Geneva shouted. She grabbed the new jar of olives Claudia had left on the table and sent it crashing to the floor. She didn't run out of the room. Rather, she surveyed the damage as if she were somehow miles above it. Then she turned slowly on her heel and walked out.

Claudia began picking up glass from the floor. I squatted down to help her. "It's okay, I can take care of this," she said. When she looked up, I saw wet stains on her cheeks. "It would be better if you went upstairs. I think Geneva needs a friend right now."

The inside of my head was like a laundry basket before the whites and darks were sorted. Claudia wasn't at all the selfish, childlike person I had expected. Instead, Geneva was the one who was having a tantrum. I didn't want to see her now. I wanted to go home.

I climbed the three flights to her room, thinking of excuses to leave. The door was ajar. When I peeked in, I saw her sitting on her bed, smoking a cigarette and staring out the window. I took a deep breath and went to sit beside her.

"You know, togetherness is not all it's cracked up to be," I ventured softly. "My brother got so sick of it that he dumped our whole family."

She sniffed. "Togetherness is something I'll never have to worry about. My father dumped me when he married Claudia."

I gently patted her hair, half expecting her to smack my hand away. But she let me continue for a few seconds, while she blew perfect smoke rings. "Want to try some yoga?" she asked finally.

"Okay, sure."

She dropped the cigarette into an open can of Coke on her nightstand and went over to her stereo. "I'll play this tape of the rain forest to get us in the mood."

Parrots squawked and water dripped while we sat on the floor, stretching and breathing rhythmically. Each new pull on my muscles felt good, like waking after a full night's sleep. I remembered how Mitch and I used to jump on his bed Saturday mornings when we were little, while Ma was still asleep. It felt like flying. One time Ma got up and saw us on her way to the bathroom, but she pretended she hadn't noticed. There was a smile on her face.

After a while, I noticed my energy beginning to return. When I caught Geneva's eye, she grinned. The room seemed lighter, even though it was turning dusk outside.

"Here, I'll show you the sun salutation. My mother taught it to me when I was only seven. She did yoga every morning . . . until she got too weak." Geneva stood on her toes, raised her arms toward the ceiling, swept them apart in a big circle, and slowly folded herself down till she dropped to her knees. Then she planted her arms on the floor, arched her back, and pulled herself forward, as if she'd just awakened from a catnap. "There's more, but we'd better stop here," she explained, rolling on her side. "It's too much to learn all at once."

More! I could hardly remember how it started. But Geneva did it with me, and I was copying her as best I could when someone laughed from the doorway. It was a man, tall and slim, with Geneva's luxurious black hair. He looked like someone in an ad for sports cars or expensive watches.

"So this is Andi," he said, winking at me. "I see you're a weirdo, too."

I sat up and smiled politely. "Not yet, but Geneva's trying to make me into one."

Geneva continued the sun salutation as if she hadn't seen her father come in or heard him speak. Or at least, I think it was the sun salutation. She had her chin and chest on the floor, and her backside up in the air, aimed right at him.

"Claude told me how disappointed you are, Gen," Mr. Peace said, still standing in the doorway. "I'm very sorry. I tried to change the date of this meeting, but the Burgesses are leaving for Florida tomorrow at noon. I have to catch them now." On the tape, a parrot laughed. Geneva sat up, legs straight out, knees together, and touched her nose to her knees. "We can reschedule your dinner for next week," Mr. Peace continued when she didn't answer.

"My birthday is today." Geneva began pointing and flexing her feet without looking at him.

"Look, there's no reason to be so difficult." A flash of anger distorted her father's face, and for a moment I was afraid he was going to slap her. But then he sighed and took a small white box with a lavender ribbon out of his suit pocket. "I really didn't forget your birthday, you know. I got this for you when I was in Los Angeles last month. I've been saving it for today."

Slowly, Geneva's head began to rise. Her eyes looked as sharp and hard as green glass shards. I wished she would talk, or shout, or even cry. Her silence was so heavy, I felt like I could barely breathe.

"Hey, come on, buddy. You know I love you." Mr. Peace came into the room and sat on her bed, holding his head in his hands as if he had a headache.

Geneva rubbed her nose on her arm and slowly lifted herself off the floor. I held my breath as she draped herself across her father's lap and laid her head on his shoulder.

I willed myself to melt into the carpet, to fly out the window, to fade into the air. I would have given anything to have been somewhere—*anywhere*—else but in that room, where Geneva had turned into someone young and spiritless.

"Careful, you're wrinkling my shirt," Mr. Peace said, shrugging his shoulder so she'd sit up. "Here, now open this." He placed the gift in her hand.

Without much interest, Geneva took the little box from his hand and opened it. She lifted out a sparkling quartz crystal on a thin silver chain.

"The woman who sold it to me said that crystals help intensify your natural powers," Mr. Peace said as Geneva examined the necklace. "Let me help you put it on." He fastened the chain around her neck.

She walked over to stand in front of the mirror. The crystal rested on her chest, gleaming and pointed like a sliver of ice. "What's the matter? Don't you like it?" her father asked, observing her unsmiling reflection in the glass.

"Sure, it's nice," she answered, rolling the crystal between her fingers, "but it's not exactly what I wished for."

Mr. Peace tugged his tie open a bit and rubbed his neck. "Well, what did you want, Geneva?" His tone had become slightly impatient.

"A guitar."

A guitar? She'd never mentioned an interest in guitars to me. I could tell from Mr. Peace's confused expression that she hadn't said anything about it to him either. He ran a hand through his hair and said, "You already have an oboe somewhere in the back of your closet."

Geneva glared into the mirror. "That was different! I thought I wanted to be in the school orchestra. You don't play the oboe in your room by yourself."

"You might if you knew how. You gave up after three weeks," her father reminded her.

Without answering, she walked over to her nightstand and picked up the photo of herself and her mother in bed. "You told me Mom played the guitar when you first met her."

"A little." Mr. Peace's tone had softened.

"Well, I want to play, too. You used to say I was just like Mom."

"But you don't even know how to read music." Mr. Peace's voice had become a little too reasonable, as if Geneva were a mental patient who claimed to be the queen of England.

I don't know how it happened, but when I looked at Geneva, I could read her mind. I felt a sinking feeling in my chest. Before she spoke, I knew exactly what her answer would be.

"I can ask Rabbi Jeff to give me lessons."

"*Who?*"

Geneva scowled at her father. "Hillside's new director of youth activities. The one who's organizing the food and clothing drive. I already told you about him when I took your old golf sweaters, remember?"

"Sure, sure. Look, if you really want it, we'll go get that guitar tomorrow. That's a promise."

She bounded across the room to hug him. "Thanks, Daddy."

He squeezed her back quickly before he extracted himself from her grasp. "Well, I've got to get going or we'll be late. Why don't I order a pizza with the works on it for you two? I'll ask for extra anchovies, okay? Nice to meet you, Andi. Good night, Geneva. I love you."

When her father was gone, Geneva fingered the crystal. "He probably bought it for Claudia." She looked out the window. The first stars had just begun to blink. "I don't care, though. I know just who I'm going to concentrate my intensified powers on."

I didn't ask. For some reason, I suddenly felt exhausted. I took the birthday present I'd bought her out of my purse and handed it over. It was a Beatles tape I'd found in the classic rock section of a record store—"Sergeant Pepper's Lonely Hearts Club Band."

14

Thanksgiving arrived for me in a battered blue van with Rabbi Jeff, wearing jeans and an old flannel shirt, at the wheel. In a way, he reminded me of my brother and his friends. Everything about them—their looks, their language, and how they acted—was so casual. I remembered how Mitchell used to beg my mother *not* to iron his shirts, and how he liked to borrow Dad's gardening sweater with the holes in the elbows. I wondered how he felt about rips and wrinkles now that he had no choice.

Anyway, it wasn't the kind of look you'd expect to see on a religious leader, even if he was wearing a yarmulke. Today R.J.'s little skullcap was orange with a brown turkey in the center. I wondered what God thought of R.J.'s funky yarmulke collection. I also wondered where they all came from. Was there a store that sold creative religious clothing, or did R.J. get his grandma to crochet them?

As I stepped up into the van, I saw Geneva and my

other Hillside classmates were already on board. "Hi, Applesauce," Jordan the joker loudly greeted me.

"Mr. Originality," I answered as I slipped in beside Geneva. But I didn't really mind being teased. I was glad to see everyone this morning.

Rabbi Jeff began humming "Turkey in the Straw" as we drove off. Geneva and I clapped our hands and tapped our feet in time to the music. Matt added a whistle and Jordan thumped his head with a fist. In the back of the van, Samantha, Karen, and Leah began snapping their fingers and giggling. It was corny, dumb, and hilarious! When we finally ran out of steam, R.J. took one hand off the steering wheel and reached for a clipboard. "I'd like you to sign up for the jobs on this list, so we can get started as soon as we arrive. Just remember, we're there to help the staff, not to get in their way. They're the generals and we're the soldiers. Geneva, would you pass this around?"

"Sure thing, Jeff."

Jeff? I'd never heard her call him by his first name before, at least not to his face. I was looking around to see if anyone else had noticed when Geneva nudged me in the side and handed me the list.

There were five possibilities:

Kitchen—food preparation
Dining room—serving
Pantry—food packing and hand out
Hard labor—carrying, lugging, toting, etc.
Cleanup—EVERYONE

Next to *Dining room—serving* Geneva had penciled in her name.

"Hey, I thought we were going to work in the kitchen together," I reminded her.

She flashed me a conspiratorial smile. "That's just what we told your mother. Don't you want to meet the people?"

To tell the truth, I didn't. What if Ma was right and the people had diseases or lice or they were violent? I wasn't sure I could cope with the Heavenly Vittles clientele. I mean, even back in nursery school, if a kid with a runny nose touched my graham cracker, I wouldn't eat it. I'd seen the city's winos and bag ladies before, and to put it politely, a little grooming wouldn't have hurt them. Just thinking about them made me feel itchy all over.

"I think I'm better at food preparation . . . like my mother," I told her.

"Forget it. I'm not going to let you hide in the kitchen." Geneva wrote my name alongside her own. I knew better than to argue.

From the seat behind us, Matt leaned forward. "Don't worry, you've got me to protect you." His arm dangled over the back of our bench and down my shoulder. It looked so pathetically skinny that I knew if anything happened, *I'd* have to protect *him*. I wondered if he'd ever fill out into a solid, comforting shape like my brother or Rabbi Jeff had. It seemed doubtful.

Geneva looked at his hand on my shoulder and then at me and wrinkled her nose in distaste. Heat rose up my neck. Suddenly I felt like there was a wad of gum on my shoulder instead of Matt's hand. I whirled around and snapped, "Will you please get out of my space!"

He jerked back like he'd just put his finger in an electric socket. "What's bugging you, anyway?"

I turned away without answering. The van pulled up in front of a low concrete building with a hand-painted sign over the door that read HEAVENLY VITTLES—A NEIGHBORHOOD NUTRITION CENTER. It was flanked by other small buildings: a grocery with a sign that read BODEGA on the left and a small redbrick church on the right. In the early morning quiet, it all looked very ordinary.

Inside Heavenly Vittles, Thanksgiving was already under way. Long rows of tables were lined with paper place mats decorated with turkeys. Every few feet, a shiny tomato-juice can held an arrangement of yellow and orange chrysanthemums. Across the back of the room, a cafeteria-style counter was stacked with brown plastic trays.

A small curly-haired man was mopping the floor. He looked up and grinned as we piled through the door. When he spotted R.J., his black eyes crinkled like raisins. "Hey, Jeff, man! Is this your crew?" He put down his mop and dried his hands on his jeans. The warmth he radiated seemed to fill up the place.

"Julio!" The rabbi and Julio knocked their fists together in the kind of greeting you see in Eddie Murphy movies. "We brought you a little gift, man." R.J. jerked a thumb behind him at the cartons full of food and clothing.

"Hey, man, we can sure use it. With the center closing

early tonight, it'll be a big help to be able to send the guests home with care packages."

"Well, we've got a nutritionally complete collection here, man," R.J. announced proudly. "Soup, tuna fish, macaroni, canned veggies, fruit, juice, et cetera, et cetera."

Julio whistled admiringly. "Wow, man! You're more organized than the army."

If either of them said *man* one more time, I was going to scream.

"Well, you can thank the gang here for that, especially Geneva." R.J. laid a hand on her shoulder. "She practically managed our food drive single-handedly. This past week, she's spent every afternoon sorting, packing, and phoning members of our congregation for donations."

"What?" I whispered. Geneva hadn't mentioned a thing about it. I turned to catch her eye, but she was staring modestly at the floor, lashes brushing her cheekbones. If she heard me, she didn't react.

I forced myself to pay attention to Julio, who was explaining that we would open at ten. The thought of eating turkey first thing in the morning made my stomach turn, until he reminded us it was the only meal some people would get that day.

After our orientation, Matt, Jordan, Geneva, and I were turned over to the "kitchen monster," a teeny woman named Gracie. She came up to my forehead and couldn't have weighed more than eighty pounds, but Gracie was a no-nonsense person. "We've got turkey, cranberry sauce, stuffing, green beans, and potatoes," she said, lifting the covers off the steaming metal pans lined up behind the cafeteria counter. "Put two slices of meat, a spoon of gravy, and one scoop of everything else on each plate. There are two choices for dessert: pumpkin or apple pie. Any questions?"

"What if they want pumpkin *and* apple pie?" Geneva asked. She was rubbing her crystal furiously between her thumb and forefinger.

Gracie's steel gray eyes pinned her to the wall. "Honey, we're going to try to serve three hundred meals today. You start going soft, and you'll be hurting more people than you're helping."

Geneva nodded seriously, as if she understood. But once she was on the front lines, I doubted she would resist any request.

"One last thing," Gracie added. "We work in two-hour shifts with a half-hour break. At noon, you kids take a rest and get something to eat. The next team will take over for you. Now go on back to the kitchen and get yourselves aprons."

When Gracie walked off, Geneva turned to me and saluted. Then she spun crisply on her heel and marched through the swinging doors. I was following right behind when she suddenly stopped short, causing me to bump into her and Matt and Jordan to crash into me. "Hey," I said, laughing, "some waitress you're going to make!" But then I followed her gaze to a table in the corner where Samantha Schaeffer was sitting, chewing on a pencil and staring at a pad. Rabbi Jeff was leaning over her, so close his chin practically brushed the top of her shiny blond head. She could probably feel his breath through her hair.

"What are you doing?" Geneva demanded.

The two of them looked up. "We're trying to stretch two hundred care packages for three hundred people," Rabbi Jeff told her.

"Don't you think you should ask me? I collected most of it."

"You signed up to do the serving," R.J. answered, ignoring her sharp tone.

"Yeah, well, I can do both." She strode over to the table and snatched up the pad. "This is all wrong!" she sneered, tearing off the top sheet and crumpling it up. Her face had a dark, nearly purplish cast, and her hair frizzed around her face as if it were electrically charged.

I felt like grabbing her hand and pulling her out of there. I hated to see her act so weird. But I didn't do anything. Neither did Rabbi Jeff. We all seemed frozen. Maybe if Gracie hadn't come in just then, R.J. would have thought of some wise, rabbinic thing to say. But the kitchen monster marched through the door demanding, "Where's my counter crew?" and the spell was broken.

I hurried over to a shelf full of aprons and pulled some down. Matt and Jordan each took one and cleared out. Geneva just stood there staring at Gracie.

"Well, get a move on!" the little woman commanded.

Geneva tossed Samantha's pad back down on the table, grabbed an apron, and stormed out of the kitchen.

15

*O*ut in the dining room, the guests were already lining up. Matt was stationed at the turkey, Jordan at the cranberry sauce and stuffing, and Geneva at the green beans and potatoes. That left me with the pies. My first customers were a family of five: two parents and three cute little kids. "Happy Thanksgiving. You can choose apple or pumpkin pie," I told them. My voice sounded unnatural to my ears.

"Whatever you've got, we're not choosy. But apple would be nice for the kids," the woman answered. While I slid their plates across the counter, she went on talking. "I always make my own turkey, but we got burned out of our apartment three weeks ago. With Cal out of work—he's a good mechanic, only his boss sold the garage—all we've been able to find so far is a room to rent. But there's no cooking allowed." She seemed anxious for me to understand that she hadn't always lived this way.

"I'm sorry," I mumbled lamely.

"Oh, don't worry about us. We'll get by," the woman answered cheerfully. Cal, her husband, just stared at his hands.

The line grew longer quickly, and there wasn't much time for conversation with the guests. In a way, that made it easier not to have to think about the awful reasons they were here today. But I couldn't help noticing the old man with hazy eyes and rotten teeth who announced that he was Donald Trump's father. "He took my money. He threw me out. He even stole my shoes!" the old man bellowed.

"You're a liar!" a woman right behind him shouted. "I'm Donald's mother, and I don't know you!"

What really amazed me, though, was how normal most of the guests were, and how incredibly grateful. Even though I'd read all those articles R.J. had passed out in class, I wasn't expecting people who looked like my neighbors, or my dad's customers, or my classmates. I didn't keep count, but I must have received hundreds of blessings. They made up for the lie I'd have to tell my mother later when she asked exactly what I'd done here. As I doled out pie, feeling happy and peaceful, I realized how foolish I'd been to be afraid of these people. Stereotyping them as violent and disease-ridden was like branding the women of Salem as witches or the Jews of Nazi Germany as devils. My fear had been nothing more than a form of ignorance . . . *prejudice*.

I wished I could share my feelings with someone. Geneva was right next to me, but I was afraid she'd think it all sounded juvenile. I might have been able to confide

122

in Matt, except he was still sore at me for snapping at him in the van. I decided the person I really needed to talk to was my brother. I'd have to call him tonight after my parents were asleep.

I was so lost in thought that at first I didn't notice the stringy old woman standing before me. "Oh, sorry," I apologized. "Would you like apple or pumpkin?"

Her pale eyes darted back and forth like silverfish. She leaned forward and whispered, "Scraps."

"Excuse me?"

She smoothed back a few strands of colorless hair and unbuttoned her baggy coat. An unpleasant odor made me draw back, but she leaned over the counter, pointing at something inside the coat. I saw it was a homemade pocket she'd tacked onto the lining. The pocket was stuffed with a plastic container. "I just need some scraps for my cats. They'll eat practically anything you've got."

"I'm just serving pie," I mumbled stupidly. "Maybe you could ask in the kitchen."

Gracie was suddenly standing behind me. She must have had supernatural hearing. "I'm sorry, but we don't feed animals. We've got too many people to worry about."

The old woman plucked nervously at her chin. "I just wanted . . ." Her voice trailed off without finishing. I watched her take her tray over to a table, knowing that she would pack most of her meal for the cats anyway. She was so thin, her skin hung like cloth on her neck.

There was no use arguing with Gracie; I already knew how she felt about "going soft." But I was overcome by the feeling that I had to do something. As soon as Gracie's attention was turned elsewhere, I asked Geneva to say I'd gone to the bathroom. Then I sneaked off to the back of the kitchen, where the remains of the guests' plates had been scraped into garbage cans.

For a few seconds, I just stared into the barrels, eyeing chewed-up turkey bones that were covered with dollops of leftover cranberry sauce and potatoes. It was pretty ugly. I took a deep breath, forced my hand into a can, and fled into the bathroom with a greasy handful.

Working quickly, I pulled bits of meat and skin from the bones and placed them in a napkin. I could see myself in the mirror over the sink, but it was as if I were watching someone else, someone who was not repulsed by other people's garbage, someone who wanted to make a strange old woman happy. When I'd filled two bundles, I washed my hands with the hottest water I could stand. Then I pressed my forehead against the glass and stared into my eyes. Before today, Thanksgiving had meant hanging out with my family, squabbling over the TV with Mitchell, playing endless games of Monopoly, setting the table with good china and cloth napkins, and eating too much. Now there would always be another meaning, too. I don't know why I started to cry.

After I slipped the old woman her scraps, I returned to dishing out pie. At twelve o'clock, Samantha, Karen, and the Tamir boys took over for us. Matt and Jordan piled up two plates and joined a group of old men at one of the tables. When he caught me watching, Matt motioned me over. I was glad he wasn't angry at me anymore, but I needed some quiet time. I waved at him and headed into the kitchen.

There was a small table for the staff, the same one where Samantha and Rabbi Jeff had cozied up. I plopped down in a chair, laid my head on the Formica top, and closed my eyes for a moment. When I opened them again, a cup of apple cider was sitting in front of me. I looked up into Gracie's appraising stare. "Where's your girl-friend?"

"Still out there serving, I guess."

"Hmm." She disappeared out the kitchen door and came back with Geneva in tow. "Time for your break."

"But I'm not tired." I could tell by the flush in her cheeks that Geneva was wired.

"Nothing doin'." Gracie pointed her at a chair. "You overexhaust yourself, you start making mistakes. Trip-ping, dropping, spilling—you could hurt someone besides yourself. Sit down and take your break. Your friends will cover for you." Reluctantly, Geneva dropped into a chair. Gracie poured her a cup of cider, too. "Now how about a piece of apple pie?" She brought a slice for me and one for Geneva and disappeared out front.

I never wanted to see apple pie again, but Geneva popped a bite into her mouth. "So, did you catch any communicable diseases yet?" she mumbled.

"Very funny." I didn't say anything about the old woman and the cat scraps. Suddenly I noticed something. "Hey, what happened to your crystal?"

She patted the empty space on her chest. "I gave it away."

"You what?"

"One of the little girls out there liked it."

"So you gave it to her?"

"Her name is Crystal," Geneva said, as if that were a logical explanation for giving it away. She put both hands flat on the table and leaned toward me. "She needs that necklace more than I do."

I felt a hot sting behind my eyes, like a warning. I wasn't sure if it was for a family that had been burned out of its home, or for an old woman whose cats were her life, or for Geneva, who understood the meaning of Thanksgiving.

But the door swung open and Rabbi Jeff burst into the kitchen, saving me from more tears. When he saw us, he dragged a chair over to the table and sat down. "It's going great out there!" he crowed. "Every day should be Thanksgiving in America." He acted as if the little scene Geneva had created earlier never took place.

Geneva swallowed a last forkful of pie. "We could at least have Thanksgiving twice a year."

Rabbi Jeff watched her closely.

"Well, it wouldn't exactly be Thanksgiving," she went on. Her cheeks were becoming quite pink, and her speech was picking up speed. "But the food drive at Hillside doesn't have to end. We could keep it going and make another delivery down here in the spring. And maybe the group that brings it can stay to help out." She looked almost shy as she searched Rabbi Jeff's face for approval.

He threw an arm around her and pulled her close. "Geneva Peace, you're one beautiful human being."

16

*W*hen I was certain my parents were asleep, I dialed Mitchell's number, which was also the number of four other people who shared his tiny apartment near Penn State. Last spring, when I'd asked Mitch if I could come for a weekend visit, he'd told me the place was really too crowded. He'd sounded sorry and kind of sad when he said it. At least he had a regular place to sleep, though. Some of the Heavenly Vittles clients didn't even have that.

It was nearly midnight. His phone rang twenty-two times before someone picked up. Mitchell wasn't home anyway, and whoever I talked to sounded groggy and irritable, so I didn't leave a message. Then I did something I hadn't done since I was a little kid: I prayed.

Naturally, with all the years of Hebrew school I'd been through, I'd said plenty of prayers. But they were the ready-made variety. The kind of praying I'd given up for a while was the personal type, the kind where you ask God to help you deal with the problems in your life, like letting my brother know that I needed him at home sometimes.

At ten-fifteen the next morning, the phone woke me up. I listened to it ring a long time, waiting for someone else to answer. No one did, so I stumbled out of bed and jerked the receiver off the hook. "Hello?"

"Andi, it's me, Mitchell."

I was kind of freaked out. I hadn't expected God to be such a fast worker. "Is everything all right?" I whispered.

"Yeah. I just wanted to see how your Thanksgiving was."

Mitchell sounded like his regular self, but I was still pretty suspicious. He never called home just to talk. "It was the usual. Ma cooked everything in the house that was edible. I hid the goldfish from her, just in case. I think she's out shopping already. She's probably restocking for next Thanksgiving."

"What about Dad?"

"He ate it all and fell asleep in front of the TV. I guess I slept late this morning. He must have left for Walloping Wallcoverings by now. If you're so interested, why didn't you come home?" I could feel my heart start beating quicker as I said the words.

"I couldn't face the hassle. You know how it is."

"What hassle?" I demanded. "Eating dinner with your family? Playing Monopoly with your only sister? Acting like you're interested in knowing whether I'm still a freak at school or if I've got a boyfriend? Sharing a few measly details about your secret life? What?"

"C'mon, Andi, you know what it's like having Ma

128

and Dad give you the third degree about everything all the time! I can't stand how Ma always cooks enough food for a family of ten and irons every piece of clothing I own and insists on vacuuming my room every day. All that concern and comfort is just a trap so she can run our lives."

"I suppose you think you've given up comfort and security." I hadn't intended to argue with him, but I couldn't stop myself. "You have no idea what real hardship is!"

"And you do?"

"No." Now that I finally had an opportunity to talk to my brother, it looked like I was going to blow it. I forced myself to concentrate on what I really wanted to say. "Listen, Mitch, yesterday I went to the city to help serve Thanksgiving meals at a soup kitchen. I'd always thought the people who came to those places were different somehow. Like they didn't love their families or want to work . . . or need the same things that we need. But they were just regular people. If Dad lost the store, we could be down there. It was easier when I still believed they weren't like us. That way, what happened to them couldn't happen to me."

Mitchell's low whistle rang in my ear. "Don't you think you're overreacting?"

"It was scary," I whispered.

Neither of us spoke for a few seconds. Then Mitch said, "The world is a scary place. That's what you learn when you get out here."

Maybe he was right, but I also knew there was more. I remembered how good I'd felt at Heavenly Vittles, giving scraps to the old woman for her cats, and how the guests were cheerful and grateful even though they had to eat Thanksgiving dinner at ten in the morning. "The world's a nice place, too, when people stick together. *Including families,*" I told him. Then I added, "Sometimes I need to talk to you, Mitch."

"Yeah, I know. I'll try to come home soon. Really." I wondered if he meant it this time. "Uh, is there anything else you want to talk about now?"

I took a deep breath and plunged ahead. "Well, there's this new rabbinic intern at Hillside. He's pretty cute, and I think this friend of mine is falling in love with him." For once I was glad I didn't have to look Mitch in the eyes. "Do you think it's possible that a twenty-four-year-old almost-rabbi would be interested in a fifteen-year-old girl?"

"Andi, I'm nineteen and I'm not interested in fifteen-year-old girls. You should try to find someone your own age."

"It's not me!" I protested. "It's my friend. Really!"

"Look, it's perfectly normal for adolescents to have crushes. In eighth grade I had one on my French teacher, Madame Belle. I used to hide outside her room and pretend to bump into her between classes."

"Is that why you won the French award at graduation?" I teased.

"To tell you the truth, I think it was all those years of eating Ma's double-egg whole-wheat *French toast.*"

For a moment, it felt like old times between us. I wished I could reach out and punch him in the arm.

"Hey, this call must be costing you a fortune," I suddenly remembered. "Want me to get off?"

He was so quiet, I thought we'd been disconnected. But then he said, "Well, actually, I've got a favor to ask you."

"Sure, anything."

"Have you got any money? A couple of weeks ago I got laid off at the station, and I used up my savings, which wasn't much anyway. Now my share of the rent is due, and I'm pretty low on funds." He was rushing through this speech as fast as he could. I knew it was hard for him.

"You used your savings, Mitch? I thought Ma and Dad said they weren't going to pay your tuition next year. How're you going to go back to school?"

My brother emitted a sigh that made me shudder. "That was just dumb talk, Andi. It wasn't real. If I worked day and night at the station, I couldn't afford the tuition here. Maybe I could squeeze through at a community college, but only if I had a job."

There was a catch in my throat that made it hard for me to speak. "Wh-what are you going to do?"

"I don't know yet. I think I've got something lined up at a pizza joint, but it doesn't pay much."

"Mitchell, you were going to be a sportswriter!"

"So if pizza tossing becomes an Olympic event, I'll be right there to cover it."

"Don't joke!" I shouted at him. "It's not funny!" For the first time, I thought I understood the meaning of having a broken heart. There was an ache in my chest that wasn't indigestion, and I was probably too young for a heart attack.

"What do you think I should do?" my brother asked quietly. His teasing tone had disappeared.

I was speechless. This was the conversation I'd thought about for months, but never did I dream my big brother would really ask me for advice. Although the answer was something I wished for every day, I took my time before I replied, "Make up with Ma and Dad."

A little bit of the old fight came back into his voice. "Things would have to be different between us."

I reached over to my dresser and stuck my hand inside my Knowledge Bowl trophy, a deep silver cup I'd filled with jelly beans. I picked one out and studied it in my palm. It was green, my lucky color. "You can't change anything if you stay away, Mitch. Come home for a visit. Just try it. *Please.*"

"Yeah, maybe you're right. Let me chew on it for a little while, okay?"

"Promise?"

"Yeah. You know, you ought to think about being a lawyer." His voice was filled with affection. But I knew my brother too well to take much credit for softening him up. He was as stubborn as Ma, and unless he'd already been thinking about coming home, he wouldn't have agreed to consider it. I hugged my pillow as hard as if it were Mitch. Suddenly, I remembered something.

"Mitchell? I've got fifty-seven dollars saved. I could send you fifty. Will that help for now?"

"Sure! I'll pay you back as soon as I can. Listen, can

you get a money order from the post office and send it today . . . without Ma or Dad knowing?"

I was already tugging off my pj's. "I'm on my way. Just remember your promise."

After I hung up, I raced around the room throwing on my clothes. If I didn't get out before my mother returned from shopping or wherever she was, she'd want to know where I was going, why, with whom, for how long, and how I was getting there and back. She'd probably insist on driving me, too. My plan was to leave her a note saying I was out with Geneva.

I already had my jacket on when the phone rang. I was going to ignore it, but it kept on ringing and ringing. What if it was Mitchell again?

"Where were you?" Geneva asked when I picked up.

"On my way out. I've got to get to the post office and send my brother a money order before my mother finds out."

"Why?"

"He can't pay his rent. I think he's afraid his room-mates will throw him out. Listen, I've got to go now. I'll talk to you when I get back."

"Wait! How're you getting there?"

"The bus."

"That could take forever. I'll be right over to get you."

"No, don't! What if my mother sees you drive up?"

"Don't worry, I'm not going to pull into the driveway. I'll wait on the corner."

In a way she reminded me of Ma, who wouldn't take no for an answer either. It was a pretty weird association.

"I don't think so. I'm really in a hurry, Geneva."

"Just wait on the corner by the bus stop," she insisted. "If it comes before me, you can take it."

Our last ride together flashed before me like a piece of a bad dream. I couldn't afford any complications now. "No, really, don't bother. The bus runs pretty frequently."

. . .

By the time I reached the bus stop, I was as nervous as Jell-O. If Ma saw me, I'd never get the money order, and Mitchell would be eating his meals at a soup kitchen. I hoped the one near him was as nice as Heavenly Vittles.

Fifteen minutes ticked by, and there wasn't a bus in sight. I was checking my watch for the millionth time when a familiar car pulled up at the curb. "Quick, get in," Geneva said, grinning from ear to ear.

I took a last look up the street and sighed. "Okay. If you take a right at the next corner, you can follow that road right into town."

The second I closed the door she took off, making the tires screech wildly. I clenched my teeth and prayed until my house was safely out of sight, but Geneva seemed not to notice. "Guess what song Jeff played for me last night?" she asked as we barreled down the road.

The last time I'd seen her we were on our way home from Heavenly Vittles in R.J.'s blue van. And although our rabbinic intern was pretty amazing, even he couldn't drive and play the guitar at the same time. I was totally confused. "You started your guitar lessons last night? On Thanksgiving?"

"Well, not exactly. But since I was the last one to get

dropped off, I invited him in to see the new guitar my dad got me."

R.J. had actually been in her house. I was really impressed. Geneva seemed to be able to make people do whatever she wanted. "So I guess he got to meet your father and Claudia," I said, trying to imagine the strange grouping.

"No, they were out shopping. Claudia forgot the turkey or something. Besides, he couldn't have played this song when they were around." She shot me a meaningful look. "It was 'Yellow Is the Color of My True Love's Hair.' " When I didn't say anything, she added, "You know, the folk song."

"Oh." I faintly remembered the song, but I didn't see the significance. Geneva was still watching me expectantly, so I joked, "I guess you'll have to put blond highlights in your hair next."

"Very funny." She brushed a lock back off her forehead. "Really, what do you think?"

What I thought was that I wanted to avoid this discussion, especially while she was driving, so I said, "It's got a nice melody."

"Not about the song, about the meaning!" she insisted, veering around a garbage truck.

We were passing all the other cars on the street. I wished she'd slow down. "Maybe it's just a song to him, not a personal statement," I said as carefully as I could. "I mean, it's hard to find a song that's not about love. He could have just chosen something he knew how to play."

Geneva sucked her lips in so tightly they turned whitish. "No, you're wrong. It was definitely a message. Just forget it, will you?" She sighed loudly and reached over to the glove compartment. "Do me a favor and feel around in there for the smokes."

"I thought you were quitting."

"I am. I'm cutting down gradually." She held out her palm for a cigarette. It made me nervous to have her driving one-handed, so I gave her one without debating the issue. She held the car's lighter to the end and drew in a long, deep breath.

In school last year, our health-ed teacher had told us that the lungs of nonsmokers could grow black just from breathing in other people's smoke. I stared through the windshield, worrying about this dismal fact, when I realized there was a red light ahead. Meanwhile, Geneva was trying to get the lighter back into its hole on the dashboard.

"Geneva, stop!" I shouted.

She looked up and jammed on the brakes. The car jerked sharply and skidded a few feet before we squealed to a halt in the middle of the intersection. On the right, a car was headed directly for us. I screamed in horror—just before it stopped, inches away. The driver blasted his horn and shouted curses from the window. But miraculously, instead of getting out of his car to chew Geneva out further, he maneuvered around us and drove away.

"Oops, sorry!" Geneva murmured as she threw the car into reverse and backed up to the corner. When the light turned green again, she took off noticeably slower.

I waited till my heart slowed down before I spoke.

"Maybe you ought to stop driving around without a license," I ventured carefully. "One of these days you're going to get caught . . . or killed."

"So?"

"So I just don't want anything to happen to you, that's all." I didn't want to offend her, especially not while she was still driving. "I mean, I appreciate this, Geneva, but you could get in a lot of trouble."

"Will you quit worrying so much!" she commanded irritably. But a few seconds later, she changed her tone. "Hey, I didn't mean to snap like that. I guess I'm just *difficult*, like my dad says." With her left hand, she punched the steering wheel lightly. "I even gave my mother a hard time the year she died."

"You were only nine," I reminded her. "All little kids can be a pain."

"Yeah, but I was a real pip. I wouldn't go to sleep when she told me to and I refused to wash my hair for months. I wouldn't even eat unless she came down to the table, which must have been hard for her. When she went into the hospital, she used to call me every night, but all I did was whine on the phone."

My lungs ached like they were on fire. "You were too young to understand how sick she was," I whispered. "You only acted like every other kid that age. When I was nine, I sprayed hair spray all over Mitchell's baseball glove so the ball would stick on the day of an important game. I was mad at him because I thought he was ignoring me."

That made Geneva smile. "You know, you're lucky to have a brother," she said with cheerfulness I knew she didn't feel. "You guys must be pretty close. What's he like, anyway?"

I kept one eye on the road and the other on the rearview mirror while I considered what to say. "He's weird and annoying and special. Like, I got the chicken pox when I was ten, and it was a really awful case. I had blisters down my throat and under my eyelids, and for a week I just stayed in bed with the curtains pulled so it wouldn't be too bright. Every day after school, Mitchell would come into my room and try to make me laugh, only nothing seemed funny. Finally one day he came in with a pair of my mother's panty hose upside down on his head, so he looked like a rabbit with long ears. He said it was the only time in my entire life that I'd see him in women's underwear, and I'd better laugh now. Once I got started, I couldn't stop."

Geneva's laughter erased the tension from the air. I couldn't help thinking that Mitchell would like her. When we pulled up in front of the post office, I jumped out, fingering the cash I'd shoved in my pocket.

"Andi, wait, I almost forgot something!" Geneva called through the window.

I sprinted back to the car. "What?"

She held up a handful of bills. "Send this to your brother."

"I can't take your money, Geneva."

"No, really!" she insisted. "There's seventy dollars here. Every time my father gives me money to order pizza, he tells me to keep the change." A sly grin appeared on her face. "How much pizza can one person eat, anyway?"

"Thanks." I took the money from her outstretched hand. "I don't know when he'll be able to repay you. With the fix he's in now, it could take forever."

She tilted her head and looked me in the eye. "I like that word, *forever*. It's so . . . dependable."

"You're crazy!" I told her, laughing. But as I headed for the post office, I thought about what she'd meant. It seemed like there was no one in her life she could count on to be there . . . except me.

As I approached the post office's glass front door, I saw a funny reflection: It was me, naturally, but over my shoulder I could also see Geneva's face poking out of the car window. For an instant it looked as if her head were actually resting on my shoulder, like I was carrying her. I took another step—and the image dissolved.

Before I went inside, I turned toward the car. "When I get back, let's go for pizza," I called to Geneva. "My treat!"

17

*B*efore this year, I'd always had trouble getting up for Sunday school at Hillside. Now I could hardly wait to find out what Rabbi Jeff had up his sleeve next. On our way home from Heavenly Vittles, he'd let it slip that he'd planned another "outing" for us. But no matter how much we'd pleaded, he wouldn't say what it was.

I got my father to drop me off at eight-thirty, a half hour early. Hillside was empty and quiet, except for the twangy sounds of Rabbi Jeff tuning up his guitar. My feet echoed on the steps as I flew up to the second floor. The thought that I'd be the first one in class made me happy. In the corridor, I slowed to a walk, so I wouldn't look overanxious.

Even before I turned the corner to our classroom, I heard their voices. Peering around the doorframe, I could see Rabbi Jeff and Geneva sitting side by side on top of his desk. She had her new guitar on her lap and was plucking at the notes of some tune I didn't recognize. R.J. had his arm around her shoulders and his hand over hers on the neck of the guitar. "No, your pointer goes here, on the E string," he said as I stood silently in the doorway.

"I can't, it won't move!" Geneva complained. They both laughed.

"Hold still. I'll place it for you." With the hand that was on hers, R.J. stretched her finger over to the top string. "Okay, now keep it there."

He let go of her and picked up his own guitar. "Ready, set, strum!"

"Go . . . tell . . . it . . . on . . . the . . . mounnntain!" R.J. sang as loud as if the room were full of people. Beside him, Geneva fumbled along, head bent over her instrument. The music they made was choppy but energetic. A sudden *boing* interrupted them.

"Ow! It hit me!" Geneva yelped, covering her nose with her hand. Her E string dangled loose from the guitar.

"You must've strummed too hard. Here, let me see." He peeled her hand off her face. She looked okay to me, but R.J. stroked her nose gently. "Poor nosey," he crooned.

A slow burn started up my neck. I crept away on tiptoe and shut myself in the bathroom. Rabbi Jeff was just giving Geneva a guitar lesson, so why did I feel like I'd stumbled into something private?

I closed the cover on one of the toilets and sat down to think. Mitchell had said teenage crushes were normal, but weren't crushes supposed to be like fantasies? This hadn't been a daydream, and it hadn't exactly looked like a music lesson either. I remembered Geneva saying I should learn to read between the lines. What if she was right, and R.J. really was attracted to her? It just wasn't the way a religious leader was supposed to behave.

Out in the hall I could hear the voices of kids making their way to class. I slipped among them and walked the few steps back to R.J.'s room. If he and Geneva had noticed me before, they didn't let on. Our classroom, and everyone in it, was noisy, disorderly, and normal. Maybe I just had an overactive imagination after all.

Rabbi Jeff was at the front of the room, bouncing on the balls of his feet and looking like a little kid with a big secret. When everyone was seated, he announced, "We need to get back to our list of world problems. I think it's time we tackled sex."

That killed my overactive imagination theory. I looked around at my classmates. They were all turning blue from holding their breath.

"AIDS, overpopulation, the dropout rate—a lot of socially relevant issues fall under the heading of sex," our rabbinic intern explained as casually as if he were discussing what he ate for lunch. "And there's also the issue of your personal values to address."

Personal values? I almost laughed. Since my entire sex life consisted of one kiss with Matt Gruenwald, I didn't exactly need any. I glanced over at Geneva, who was wearing her dreamy yoga expression. The corners of her lips were curved slightly upward, and her breathing was slow and even. By the look in her eyes I could tell she was somewhere else, like on the planet Venus. Behind me, Jordan was jiggling his knee under the desk, while in front, Samantha Schaeffer twirled a strand of hair into a tight coil. I didn't dare look at Matt.

Rabbi Jeff tugged his ponytail. "Last summer, my friend

Sascha Elliott and I attended a leadership training workshop for a sex-education program called Youth and Sexuality. The purpose of the program is to provide more than just a bunch of dry facts. It's designed to help each of you develop your own moral code, so you're prepared for the real-life issues that arise. And it's a lot of fun."

The only sex education I'd had was in my seventh-grade health class. All we did was read from a textbook with little black-and-white drawings that made the reproductive organs look about as sexy as car parts. It didn't answer the kinds of questions I had, and it wasn't fun, either.

"I thought it would be great for us to try the program together," R.J. continued. "So I've arranged to take you to Paradise Path next weekend, where Sascha and I will lead Hillside's first annual Youth and Sexuality Retreat."

He held up a sheaf of papers and waved them in the air. "These are copies of a letter explaining the program to your parents. I'm also holding an informational meeting for them on Thursday night. There are permission slips here for all of you, too. Any questions?"

I had a dozen of them. Like what did you do on a sexuality retreat, and did the boys and girls do it together or separately? Like whether it would be totally embarrassing or just a little or even fun. Or what happened if you hated it and wanted to go home? But I didn't ask any of those things and neither did anyone else. No one even spoke until Matt finally broke the silence.

"What's Paradise Path?"

"It's a summer camp about two hours north of here in the foothills of the Berkshires. They've got bunks and a kitchen and all the other facilities we'll need." R.J. looked us over and grinned. "Come on, smile! You're going to enjoy this, I promise."

For the rest of the hour, we watched a video about a high school in Israel that had a special program for American students. Each American teenager was paired with an Israeli student who had been studying English, and together they were responsible for learning the day's lessons in Hebrew and English. I tried to imagine how it would be to transfer there from Barf, but at that moment, it was hard to imagine anything being more exotic than a sexuality weekend.

After class, Geneva walked me out to the driveway. "Do you think all the girls are going to bunk together?" she asked.

I decided to play dumb. "Where?"

"At Paradise Path!"

I shrugged. "It doesn't matter to me."

"What do you mean?" She put a hand on my shoulder and pulled me around so I was facing her. "You're going, aren't you?"

"You know my parents. I don't think they'll sign the permission form." The truth was, I wasn't certain I wanted to go, even if my parents would allow it.

"But you've got to go!"

"Why? You don't need me."

"What do you mean?" Geneva honestly looked puzzled.

"I thought you'd jump at the chance to spend the weekend alone with R.J.," I blurted out.

"Alone? Our whole Hillside class will be there! You

know Samantha hasn't even spoken to me since Thanksgiving. The rest of the kids ignore me, too. I'm not going without you."

"No one ignores you, Geneva," I said automatically. But I couldn't help thinking that she'd been the one to set herself apart from our classmates. Did she really believe that they'd excluded her?

She laid her hand on my arm and gave me a squeeze. "C'mon, Andi, this will be good for you."

"Name one reason."

"You need the practice."

I rolled my eyes and sighed loudly. "I don't think that's exactly what Rabbi Jeff has planned."

"Who says we can't have our own agenda? Don't you want to meet his friend Sascha? With a name like that, I bet he's one of those romantic Russian types, like Baryshnikov."

She'd said the right thing. After I'd seen him dance in the movie *The Turning Point* when I was eleven, I'd insisted that Ma enroll me in a ballet class. It only took a few months of difficult and sometimes painful lessons before I knew I'd never be a famous dancer, but I still adored Baryshnikov. Besides, wasn't a program on human sexuality the perfect place to discuss *crushes?* The program might be good for Geneva, and she'd said she wasn't going without me.

I threw my hands up in a show of surrender. "Okay! You talked me into it. But I'll have to work on my parents." Out of the corner of my eye, I saw my father's car pull into the driveway. "I guess I'll start right now."

18

My father dropped me off at home and picked up my mother at the same time. They were going to do inventory at Walloping Wallcoverings, which was easier on Sunday, when the store was closed to customers. I grabbed an apple from the refrigerator and ran up to my room. There was a message taped to my door saying Alana Voegel-Whitcroft had telephoned. It did not make me happy that Barf's most popular girl was trying to reach me. Still, it was not wise to offend Alana, so I rang her back.

"Oh, Applebomb, how was your religious experience?" she asked when she heard my voice. Alana was careful never to openly criticize, but her tone became condescending whenever the subject of my religion arose.

"Enlightening as always. What can I do for you?" I figured she wanted the math homework.

"What makes you think I called because I need something?" Alana sounded hurt. What an actress. Julia Roberts, look out!

"I'm actually calling to invite you to a party," she

continued after a few seconds of wounded silence.

I tried to sound disappointed. "Oh, gee, I'm busy next weekend." But then I couldn't stop myself from adding, "I'm going on a human sexuality retreat with my Hillside class."

"Really? What exactly is that?"

"Kind of like sex ed, I guess. You know—values, birth control, social diseases, and . . . stuff."

"Are boys going, too?"

I know it was dumb, but I wanted to impress her. "It wouldn't be much of a weekend without them," I threw out casually. At Barf, boys were always running after Alana.

"Sounds like it could be interesting. You can tell us the details at my party, which is the weekend *after* next, so you'll be able to come anyway."

"Oh, okay." Let her think I was coming. Later I'd come up with some excuse to cancel. I was pretty sure she was only inviting me because she wanted to hear more about all the driving she imagined I did. Maybe she even thought I'd drive over to her house.

"One more thing." Her voice affected a slightly apologetic tone. "It'll be just us girls. The boys at Barf are so . . ."

"*Boring*," I finished, guessing at her meaning.

"Exactly." She seemed delighted that I understood her.

I was getting ready to say good-bye when she added, "Oh, Andi, why don't you bring your friend Geneva along?"

"I'll see if she can make it."

• • •

It turned out Ma barely had any objections to my going on the retreat. All she had to say after she went to the parents' meeting R.J. held was "it sounds like a sensible program." Once I agreed to take my vitamins and my electric toothbrush along, she signed the permission slip. I ran up to my room and packed my bag before she could change her mind—even though it was only Thursday.

So when the blue van pulled up at Hillside Saturday morning, I felt more than ready for Youth and Sexuality. And Rabbi Jeff didn't waste any time. Part one—"Desensitization"—began as soon as we'd all climbed aboard. He explained that we were going to say every sex word we'd ever heard, so that by the time the ride was over, we wouldn't act like jerks whenever a private body part or a reproductive urge was mentioned. From over his shoulder, he shot a meaningful glance at the boys, who were all seated on the right side of the van.

"We'll start with a game of categories," he continued, after the groans and the snickering had died down. "The idea is to come up with as many slang expressions as you can for each word I say. It'll be boys against girls. The first is just a practice round. Ready? *Kiss.*"

"French!" Jordan immediately yelled out.

"Make out," Matt added, with a touch more restraint.

We girls just looked at each other uncomfortably. "C'mon, you're not going to let the guys beat you," R.J. urged us.

Well, what the heck? It was going to be a long ride. "Osculate," I volunteered. When my classmates stared at me, I added, "I learned it playing Knowledge Bowl." Everyone broke up laughing.

After that we started to relax. Still, I was glad when we finally got to the end of the last bumpy road. Long rides always give me a headache. Gingerly, I stepped down from the van and squinted at the summery green-and-white cottages. There were six of them planted on either side of a bigger building that had a long, inviting porch under a sloping roof. The scene reminded me of the pictures I'd seen in the camp brochures Ma used to leave on my desk when I was younger. They'd been nice pictures, but I couldn't imagine spending the summer in a cabin full of strangers. After a while she'd stopped leaving the brochures.

Geneva threw her backpack from the van and hopped out, her guitar strapped to her back. The ride hadn't bothered her an iota. "Andi, you don't look so good. You're the color of cottage cheese."

"Thanks a lot. Which cabin do you think is ours?"

Before she could guess, Rabbi Jeff was out of the van. "Girls, you're in the first bunk to the left of the main house," he said, pointing us on our way. "Boys, you're in the one to the right. They're the only two cabins equipped with heaters. When you get in, turn up the thermostat first thing. It'll take a while to get them warm. Why don't we all take an hour to unpack and get comfortable? We'll meet at four."

"I thought Sascha was going to be here," Geneva said. I was glad she'd asked, because I'd been wondering about him, too.

"*Everyone* will meet at four." R.J. clapped one hand on Matt's shoulder and the other on Jordan's and nodded at Mark, Ben, and Brad to follow. "C'mon, roomies. I hope none of you snore." The all-male band plodded off, leaving Geneva, Samantha, Karen, Leah, and me to fend for ourselves.

United by our strange surroundings, we trekked the sun-dappled path together. The crunching of leaves under our feet seemed to startle the squirrels and chipmunks into activity. Birds suddenly began chirping. I began to feel better almost immediately.

Samantha pulled open the door of our little cabin. "Looks like the seven dwarfs live here," she joked. We piled in behind her and inspected the place. It was plain and neat: seven cots in two rows, with a set of shelves behind each one. A door at the back of the room led to an oversize bathroom with toilets, sinks, shower stalls, and an assortment of dead bugs.

I turned up the thermostat and began unpacking my clothes onto the shelves behind one of the beds. I had to crawl under it to find an outlet for the electric toothbrush Ma had insisted I bring along. After I finished, I stretched out flat, still bundled in my jacket against the late-autumn chill. The sour smell of mildew wafted up from the thin mattress.

"Let's explore!" Geneva urged as soon as I was comfortable.

"No, thanks, I'm going to rest," I told her.

"So am I," Samantha agreed, plopping on the bed across from mine. "Anyway, the guys are probably outside trying to teach those sweet little animals to curse."

When I laughed, Geneva glared at me. She grabbed her guitar and left without looking back. I let her go.

I talked with Samantha for a while, and then I must have dozed off, because the next thing I knew, I was being awakened by the sound of the door slamming. Geneva was standing in the threshold, examining me through small round glasses.

Except Geneva didn't wear glasses.

"Hi, I'm Sascha," she said when she saw I was awake. I looked her over suspiciously. She was dressed in Geneva's black jeans and had her same black hair, although she'd pulled it back in a ponytail. On closer inspection, I noticed that she didn't have any purple highlights, and anyway, this person was definitely more mature—maybe twenty-one or twenty-two. Also, her face was somehow calmer than Geneva's was. Still, she looked an awful lot like Geneva. I wondered if I was still dreaming.

"Jeff sent me over," she continued when I didn't answer. "I'm your all-purpose chaperon, sex-ed counselor, and lousy cook." She wrinkled her nose at her own joke. "Where is everyone?"

I looked around and realized I was alone in the cabin. The sound of running water echoed from the bathroom. "I thought you were a guy," I blurted out. "Everyone does."

"Ohh." She smiled with her mouth closed. "I'm surprised Jeff didn't tell you anything about me. I'm the one who crochets his *kippas*," she said, using the Hebrew word for yarmulke.

She was surprised? I thought of the turkey yarmulke and the one with the music notes all around it and the lovely dark blue one that looked like the night sky.

When you knitted a sweater for someone, it meant you liked them a lot, maybe loved them even. Wasn't crocheting a kippa the same thing?

Samantha, Karen, and Leah came out of the bathroom in towels and dripped their way across the floor. "Brr, it's still freezing in here! Geneva, did you see a clothesline outsi—" Samantha stopped walking and talking at the same time.

"I thought you were Geneva," she stammered.

"This is Sascha," I explained.

"Hi." Sam looked as bewildered as I felt.

Behind her wire rims, Sascha's eyes brightened. "Did you just call me Geneva? Jeff thinks she looks like me, too! He talks so much about all of you. Let me guess who's who." She took a moment to examine each of us. "You're Andi," she told me right away.

"How'd you know?" I asked, amazed.

She laughed lightly. "You're the only one with an electric toothbrush behind your bed."

Great. Since R.J. had never seen my electric toothbrush, I could only imagine what he'd told her. That I was overprotected or that I was a perfectionist or that I was a geek. Or maybe all three.

"Who am I?" Sam wanted to know.

Sascha cocked her head and thought for a moment. "Easy. You're Samantha. You've got deep blue eyes and"—she gazed at Sam's lips—"a trace of red lipstick."

Samantha beamed with pleasure. Then she began shuffling through her enormous suitcase for something new to wear. I guess her morning outfit was dirty from the bus ride.

Sascha walked slowly around Karen and Leah, who were still in their towels. They both had medium-length brown hair, brown eyes, and no noticeable scars. "You're Karen, and you're Leah," she said, getting them both right. I was genuinely impressed.

"How'd you guess?" they squealed.

"I'm psychic," Sascha answered mysteriously. She looked around. "Now where's Geneva?"

My stomach sank like the *Titanic*. Even though the female Sascha was fun, I knew Geneva wasn't going to like her . . . or what she might mean to R.J. It was suddenly hard to find my voice. "Out for a walk," I whispered.

Sascha smiled. "I guess we'll run into her on our way to the rec room. I'm supposed to bring you girls over there in ten minutes." She tugged at the bottom corner of Karen's towel, which, I realized, was labeled with her name. "You'd better get ready."

• • •

Geneva still hadn't returned when we left for the main house to join the rest of the group. "Maybe I should wait here for her," I suggested to Sascha.

"Don't worry. She's probably found Rabbi Jeff already," Samantha butted in. "She follows him around like a lost kitten."

"Shut up, Sam!" I snapped. I banged out of the cabin and started up the path. Every noise caused me to jerk my head around and look for Geneva, but she never appeared. I wondered if she'd already heard about Sascha and had stormed off into the woods, hurt and angry. Or maybe she was hitching a ride back home by now. An image of Geneva getting into a black pickup truck made my whole body quake. Behind me, Sascha gave my shoulder a pat.

Inside the main building, I could hear the slap of paddles and the hollow bounce of a Ping-Pong ball. The sound led us to the door of a musty room with a hand-lettered sign posted above: WRECK WROOM. The boys were gathered around the Ping-Pong table, while Geneva and Rabbi Jeff sat in the center of the room, picking out a melody on their guitars. They didn't notice us come in.

"See?" Samantha whispered in my ear.

I stayed at the doorway and watched as Sascha approached them. When he saw her, R.J. stopped playing. Geneva's head popped up and followed his, as if it were attached by an invisible line. I could tell from the questioning look on her face that she still didn't suspect a thing.

Anyway, there was no need for a formal introduction. When Sascha leaned down and kissed our rabbinic intern on the lips, it was perfectly clear who she was.

19

*W*e began our first session by making out lists of our sexual expectations, which meant what we might be willing to "do" on a first date, a second date, a third date, and after going out with the same person for a month, six months, or more. Then we were supposed to list what we thought our parents would expect of us.

While everyone was writing furiously, I stared at my blank paper. It was like facing a test I'd never studied for. How could I know what I'd be willing to do if I'd never even been on a date?

I tried concentrating on the males I knew best: my brother; my dad; Matt; and Rabbi Jeff, who was now holding Sascha's hand. They were no help at all. Finally, I folded my paper in half and wrote down the left side:

My Expectations

First date: (1) Look up at the sky
                  (2) Kiss with eyes closed

Second date:	(1) Watch old movies
	(2) Kiss with eyes closed
Third date:	(1) Eat together (I think this requires a certain amount of trust. It's hard to look attractive with threads of pizza cheese hanging out of your mouth or hamburger grease dripping down your chin.)
	(2) Kiss with eyes closed
One month:	(1) Read Alfred Noyes's poem *The Highwayman* together (This is the most romantic poem ever written!)
	(2) Kiss with eyes open (which takes more courage than keeping your eyes closed)

Six months or more: Impossible to say

Everyone else was done before I even got to the "parents' side" of my paper. If we were asked to read our responses aloud, I planned to tear the page up and eat it. But after we'd completed the assignment, Rabbi Jeff had us burn them in the fire he and Sascha had started in the fireplace.

"That was an exercise to get you thinking," R.J. explained. "If you start out in life with some idea of where you're going, you won't get lost so easily. And it doesn't hurt to have your parents' map, in case you ever need a guide."

If I asked Ma, I wouldn't just get a map, I'd get an

entire atlas full of warnings about what happened to girls who kissed too soon or too much or let boys touch them in "certain places."

I have to admit I was dying to see Geneva's list. If she'd been beside me, I would have swallowed my pride and shared mine with her. But she'd chosen a seat as far away as our circle of ten would allow. When I finally caught her eye, she glared at me as if Sascha's arrival was all my fault.

"Let's do a little role-playing before dinner," Rabbi Jeff said when our sex expectations had turned to ashes. He had his arm around the back of Sascha's chair.

If you ask me, whoever invented role-playing should be shot. Since first grade, I have role-played everyone and everything, from Squanto's squaw at the first Thanksgiving to a white blood cell fighting an infection. The spontaneous dialogue is always stiff, and no one ever says what they think anyway. They're too busy trying to guess what the group leader wants them to say.

But Rabbi Jeff had these little white slips of paper with situations written on them. "We'll have two people act these out, and then we can discuss their interaction." He waved a slip in the air. "Here's a scene for two girls. Who'll volunteer to go first?"

It was a chance to talk to Geneva. I raised my hand.

"Okay, Andi, choose a partner and take a few minutes to read this over." He handed me the paper.

I tapped Geneva and headed over to a far corner of the room. "Hey, are you okay?" I whispered.

She lifted a shoulder. "Yeah, I'll live. Aren't you going

to say, 'I told you so,' Miss Know-it-all?" Her voice was filled with contempt.

"N-no, of course not." I was stunned by the anger I saw in her eyes. I unfolded the slip of paper. "We'd better look at this."

Susan's best friend, Tina, calls to ask a favor. Tina is secretly planning to stay at her boyfriend Tim's house on Saturday night. His parents are going to be away for the weekend. Tina intends to tell her mother she will be spending the night with Susan. If Tina's mother calls, will Susan cover for her?

"I'll be Tina," Geneva said. She stalked back to the circle without waiting for me to reply.

I sat on my imaginary bed while Geneva dialed an imaginary telephone. "Ring, ring!"

"Hello?" I cradled the invisible receiver to my ear.

"Susan, this is Tina. I have a little favor to ask."

"Sure, what?"

"I'm staying at Tim's this weekend while his parents are away, and the most natural thing to tell my mother is that I'll be at your house. If she calls, would you cover for me and say I'm in the shower or something? Then you could just ring me at Tim's and I'll call Mom back."

My face felt like it was on fire. It was better playing a white blood cell. "I don't know, Tina. I'm not such a great liar," I said, stalling for time.

Geneva smirked at my answer. "Look, all you'd have to say is that I'm in the shower. I'll write it down for you."

"Why?" I mumbled.

"Why what?"

"Why do you have to stay at Tim's?"

She pulled a face that let me know she thought I was totally hopeless. "We're in love. We want to be together."

Her growing impatience was making me flustered. I searched for the right words, but all I could come up with was, "You're only fifteen. Why rush?"

"You don't understand much about love, Susan. It can disappear any instant. You've got to take it when you can get it."

I could feel my old-lady look taking over my face. "Real love lasts. You have so many years ahead of you."

"I can't wait that long."

"You could get hurt!"

"It hurts to be without love!" Geneva was shouting at me.

Hot, fat tears began streaming down my face. I scrubbed them away with a hand.

"G-girls, I—I think we'd better stop here," R.J. stammered.

But Geneva just kept yelling. "Andi, why don't you grow up . . . or go home to your mommy and daddy!" She flew out of the room.

R.J. ran out after her, and Sascha came over to comfort me.

I stopped crying and crept back to my folding chair. Matt leaned over and gave my arm a pat.

"Do you think you'll be okay?" Sascha whispered in my ear. She smoothed my hair from my face gently.

I nodded. Geneva was wrong, I wasn't a baby.

"Then I think I'll see if Jeff and Geneva need me. I'll be back soon." Sascha left my Hillside classmates sitting in their circle. No one spoke or even moved.

Jordan finally broke the silence. "What's wrong with Geneva, anyway?"

"She's jealous of Sascha," Samantha announced, "and anyone else R.J. pays attention to."

Under his unruly brown mop of hair, Jordan looked puzzled. "Why?"

"Because she's in love with him, you dope! Haven't you noticed how she always glues herself to him?"

"You're crazy! He's almost a rabbi," Jordan answered, but he didn't sound so sure of himself.

Now Sam challenged me. "Tell him, Andi. Isn't it true?"

Something inside me woke, sharp and alert. "They're just friends," I said firmly. "Geneva was mad at me, that's all. She hates it when I disagree with her. We fight like this all the time. She'll be fine." I gave Samantha a look that dared her to argue.

"You guys must be a barrel of laughs together," Jordan said quietly.

Everyone laughed too hard, but I was grateful to him for the distraction.

The boys returned to the Ping-Pong table while Sam, Karen, and Leah regrouped. "I'm going out to look for Geneva," I told them. I was hurt and I was angry, but I was also worried about her.

Rabbi Jeff was just coming in when I got to the front door. "We found her. She's okay," he told me before I could ask.

160

My heart thumped a little slower. "Where is she?"

"In the cabin with Sascha . . . getting her stuff together. She wants to go home."

"What?"

R.J. put an arm around me. "Geneva's still pretty upset. I couldn't talk to her. She's calling her stepmother to come get her—her father's out of town."

"She's calling *Claudia*?"

"Yes, why?"

I shook off his arm and grabbed the doorknob. "I want to talk to Geneva."

"Not right now," he said, putting his hand over mine. "She doesn't want to see anyone. Give her some time to calm down." He looked away from me and added, "She thinks everyone she loves always deserts her."

I looked him straight in the eye and said what was on my mind. "You knew how Geneva felt about you. Everyone did. You should have told her about Sascha before."

Rabbi Jeff leaned back against the wall and closed his eyes for a moment. He looked so young; sometimes I forgot he wasn't much older than Mitchell. "Look, Andi, I made a mistake with Geneva. I knew she had a crush on me, but infatuation's a common thing for girls your age. I never expected she'd be so upset about Sascha . . . or that she was so serious about me."

"She really thought you loved her." My words came out like a reproach.

"I'm a rabbi, Andi. I care about all of you. Only, Geneva seemed to need more attention. I tried to be like a big brother to her. She's a wonderful, vivacious girl, and I loved the spirit in her." He dragged a hand down over his troubled face. "But I didn't know enough about her. Now instead of helping her, I've hurt her."

His hair was rumpled and his skin was pale. He looked so miserable that I felt kind of sorry for him. "Maybe no one can love Geneva enough," I said softly. I opened the door. "I'm going to see her."

. . .

Outside, it was twilight. Squares of yellow light illuminated the cabin's small windows. I found Sascha sitting in shadow on the front steps. "She doesn't feel like talking," she said, nodding toward the door. "How're you doing?"

I shrugged away her question. "I'm okay now." Actually, there was a pit like the Grand Canyon in my stomach.

She stood up and shoved her hands into the pockets of her jeans. "I'm really sorry about what happened back there. I had no idea—"

"I know," I interrupted. I didn't mean to be abrupt, but I knew if I waited too long, I was going to lose my nerve.

I took the deep cleansing breath Geneva had taught me when we did yoga, and I opened the cabin door. Geneva was sitting stony-faced on her cot. Somehow she looked smaller and younger than I'd remembered. "Hi," I murmured. "R.J. told me you were calling home."

Her expression didn't change. I wasn't even sure she was going to answer, but then she said, "Yeah, *Claudia's* on her way." She made Claudia's name sound like a disease.

"I just wanted to say I'm sorry about the role-playing scene. I know I got pretty personal. I shouldn't even have picked you. I knew you were upset. I just wanted us to talk."

She jerked her head impatiently. "Look, there's nothing to talk about. Just forget it, okay?"

Forget what? The scene? This trip? Our relationship? I had to know. "So we're still friends?"

Geneva looked out the window. "Yeah, sure." She could have been agreeing to anything.

I couldn't help thinking she owed me an apology, too. Although I'd made her pain worse by putting the spotlight on her, I hadn't meant to hurt her. But Geneva's attack on me had been on purpose. Still, I knew I'd have to ignore my feelings. That was just the way things were between us.

I was searching for the right thing to say—something that would keep her in my life—when I remembered Alana's phone call. "The Barf girls are having a party next Friday night. They want me to bring you. It should be a real laugh. Want to come?"

"Maybe." She was still staring out the window. I joined her and we sat there silently, long past the time it was too dark to see anything.

20

$\mathcal{I}$ waited until Thursday night to ask Geneva about the party again. Her phone rang ten times before she picked up, each ring making my heart pound harder. But when she finally answered, she sounded like her old self.

"I was painting my room," she said, explaining why it took her so long to get the phone. "It's sort of a pinkish violet. You should come over and see it."

"Okay, how about tomorrow? Then maybe afterward we could go to that Barf party together." When she didn't answer right away, I added, "I mean, if you want to. If you'd rather do something else, I won't mind."

I waited for her to think it over. "Let's go," she said. "It might be interesting."

My insides began fizzing like a bottle of seltzer. "Great! I'll be over around seven. Or I could come early and we could go for pizza. You know, I'm really glad you're not still mad."

"I told you to forget about that, didn't I?" she snapped.

"Y-yeah, sure." But I wondered when, or if, *she* ever would.

• • •

My father dropped me off at the Peaces' house so Geneva and I could walk to Alana's party together. Ma was expecting him to chauffeur us to the Voegel-Whitcrofts' house, too, but I wanted some time alone with Geneva. Once we were out of the house, Dad was easy to convince.

When she opened the door, Geneva was dressed in an old blue bathrobe. "I thought we'd get dressed together," she said, responding to my puzzled expression.

I looked down at my navy blue sweater and tan corduroy pants. "I thought I was dressed."

She fingered my sleeve with distaste. "You want to go to the party looking like a candidate for Miss Preppy America?"

I shook my head sadly. "Dressing can be a highly contagious disease. I guess I'm doomed."

"Not with Dr. Peace around. I believe you can still be helped. That is, if you want to be. Of course, we'll need to give you shock treatment. . . ."

My treatment began in Claudia's closet. Geneva's father and stepmother were away for the weekend, so everything Claudia had left behind was temporarily ours. Geneva confessed that she'd told her dad she was staying with me, so she wouldn't have to put up with the Chernovs again.

Claudia had a lot of silky, clingy clothes. "Here, I think red's a good color for you," Geneva said, tossing me a scarlet satin cowgirl shirt. Along the yoke was a fringe of long black tassels, and its buttons were fake pearl studs.

I put the shirt on. "What do you think?"

Geneva stuck her head out of the closet and gave me the once over. "It doesn't work with those pants." She pulled something off a hanger. "Try this."

She held out a microscopic black satin skirt. Although Claudia was at least two inches taller than me, I couldn't believe it would even cover my rear end. The whole outfit must have been left over from her wilder days. I wriggled into it and headed for the mirror. I looked like a cocktail waitress.

"It's perfect!" Geneva proclaimed.

For herself, she chose a short, slithery black dress with a low neckline and a pair of Claudia's four-inch heels. In front of the mirror, she piled her hair up on her head and fixed it with a rhinestone barrette. She reminded me of a sleek black panther, wild and a little dangerous.

"Something's missing," she announced, opening Claudia's dresser next. As she bent over the drawer, I noticed the back of her neck. It was the first time I'd seen it since I'd highlighted her hair. "Hey, what happened to your wish braid?" I exclaimed.

"Oh, I cut it off," she said, as she tossed combs and beads and lacy underthings onto the floor. "I decided it was really dumb."

My hand flew under my hair to my own wish braid, but Geneva didn't notice. Did she even remember that she'd made one for me? When she spun around, she was holding up a lipstick case. "The finishing touch," she announced.

We drew on racy red mouths and left for Alana's house.

• • •

166

Geneva's slow steps in Claudia's spike heels made us the last ones to reach the Voegel-Whitcrofts'. As we unbuttoned our jackets in her front hall, Alana took in our outfits jealously. She flashed a smug smile at Bonita Dickerson, who passed it on to Deidre Van Dorne, Caroline Tittle, and Phoebe Porter. "I told you Andi and her friend knew how to party."

We followed them through the empty house—Alana's parents were out—and into her room, which had a nautical motif. The headboard of her bed was a highly polished ship's wheel, and the walls were painted ocean blue with a border of waves running around the top. A silver-framed photo of Alana, taken on the deck of a sailboat, sat on her desk. It all reminded me of restaurants decorated like Mexican villas or the Hawaiian islands. Everything was bright and clean and fake.

"We're just dying to hear about your sex retreat," Alana said when Geneva had been introduced to everyone.

We were lounging on the soft sand-colored carpet. Geneva shot me a slantwise glance with just the slightest hint of a smile, nothing the others would notice. I answered with a blink that lasted a quarter second longer than normal. Then I propped my chin up on an arm and let her do the talking.

"Oh, it was just the usual stuff, safety, self-control, peer pressure, you know."

She flicked some invisible lint off her black dress.

Caroline's baby-doll face settled into a pout. "Wasn't there anything fun?"

"I guess you could say the role-playing was interesting."

"Role-playing what?" Bonita prodded.

"Lots of different situations."

"Well, what did you two act out?"

Geneva sighed loudly, as if to remark on Bonita's lack of imagination. "Andi, why don't you describe our scene?"

I cleared my throat to rid it of the lump that was stuck there, but my voice still came out like a croak. "It was about this girl who was thinking of staying at her boyfriend's house when his parents were away," I began slowly.

"And?" Alana asked impatiently.

"I don't remember exactly. It's hard to describe." I wished Geneva hadn't brought up the role-playing at all. It was still so painful to remember, I wondered how she could act so cool about it. I was beginning to feel that attending this party was a big, fat mistake.

The Barfettes shot each other looks of contempt at my dull response. But after a moment, Alana said, "Why don't we try one?"

"Without boys, it's not going to be very exciting," Caroline grumbled.

Geneva twisted her bracelets thoughtfully. "Some of us could dress like guys. I always dress up when I want to be inspired."

"In what?" Already bored, Alana was inspecting the tips of her pale hair for split ends. "I haven't got any men's clothes."

Geneva arched her eyebrows and smiled tantalizingly. "Ah, but you have your father's wardrobe. I'll bet you could outfit an entire Girl Scout troop with his things."

Alana hesitated a moment. Maybe she was uncomfortable about invading her parents' room or thinking about whether we'd wrinkle her father's shirts and suits. But it didn't take her long to overcome her reservations. She jumped up suddenly and flicked back her hair. "All right, follow me."

If Alana's room was a sailboat, her parents' room was an ocean liner. An enormous platform bed dominated its center. Dark wood cabinets with highly polished brass handles ran along three walls, and the sea green carpeting looked as if it had never been stepped on until we waded across to reach the walk-in closet.

While the others fingered shirts and jackets, I kept my eyes on the door. What if Alana's parents returned home early and found us plundering their closet? All around me, shoes and ties began flying. Obviously, I was the only one worried.

"We'll need three or four boys to play our scenes," Geneva directed. "I'll be one." She unzipped her dress and let it drop to the floor. "Does anyone want to wear this?"

"I do!" Caroline answered right away.

Bonita, Deidre, and Alana decided to be boys, too, which left the girls' roles to Caroline, Phoebe, and me. Alana offered Phoebe one of her mother's glitzy dresses, but Phoebe insisted on staying in her own clothes. It was a secret relief to know I wasn't the only one who was uneasy.

Dressing in Dr. Voegel-Whitcroft's suits, ties, and heavy shoes seemed to effect some magical transformation in Alana and her friends, as if they'd changed skins as well. They became louder and more physical, poking and jabbing each other the way boys do. They tied back their hair and rubbed lime-scented after-shave into their cheeks. Then they pushed each other out of the way to pose in front of the closet's mirrored doors, which gave Alana the idea to take pictures.

"Pair off," she ordered, pointing a camera at us.

Geneva, decked out in gray pinstripes, grabbed Caroline by the arm and stepped forward, grinning. She leered wolfishly at Caroline, the way I imagined Kenny McKenna might. Caroline caught hold of Geneva's necktie and put it between her teeth. The flash from Alana's camera made them both squint.

Bonita grabbed me for a picture next. She threw an arm around my shoulder and planted a kiss on my cheek, holding it until Alana snapped. We horsed around that way for a while, collapsing with laughter at each other's boldness.

We never got into the kind of role-playing Rabbi Jeff had conducted, but this was a lot more fun. Things weren't turning out so badly after all. I looked around at everyone having a great time and felt proud to be Geneva's friend.

"Got anything to drink?" Geneva asked Alana as she opened her collar and loosened her tie. "These men's clothes are murder on the sweat glands."

"Sure." We traipsed out to the kitchen, where Alana threw the refrigerator door wide open. "What'll it be?"

Geneva swaggered over to the table and plopped heavily into a chair. "Make mine a beer."

Alana's eyes lit up. "Really?"

"At home I always drink beer with my dad."

I'd never seen her drink anything stronger than coffee. Still, it wasn't hard to imagine Geneva talking her father into letting her have a beer.

Alana pulled out a six-pack of tall brown bottles and passed them around. The "boys" were the first to open theirs.

"Well, bottoms up!" Geneva toasted us with her bottle before she chugged it down. Her cheeks were flushed with heat and excitement. In the wool pin-striped jacket, with her tie askew, she looked surprisingly pretty.

Bonita and Deidre each lifted theirs and took a swig, but I noticed Alana was only touching the bottle to her lips. "Come on, girls, drink up!" Geneva snapped when she caught me looking.

Caroline reached for the opener, but I left my bottle on the table. I'd tasted my father's holiday wine, and I remembered the warm, dreamy feeling it gave me. If just a few sips could make me respond that way, I wondered what effect a bottle of beer would have. It might feel good, but on the other hand, I might end up staggering in the street. Besides, what if someone came in and caught us? I could never face my parents. No, I'd already given up driving illegally; I was definitely not going to start drinking illegally.

"I'm not in the mood," I said.

Alana took a big, slow gulp before she answered me. "You've probably never even tried it, Applebomb."

"Are you kidding?" Geneva answered for me. "Andi's

brother always shares his beer with us." She grabbed my bottle. "Here, I'll have yours."

I had to clasp my hands to keep from snatching it back, but the others were grinning approvingly, except for Phoebe, who, I realized, had quietly moved her untouched beer into her lap.

"I'm starving," Geneva announced, wiping her mouth with the back of her hand. "What else is in the fridge?"

Alana pulled open the door and stuck her head back inside. "Anchovies, tofu, celery, oat bran . . . my mother never buys anything you can eat."

"No ice cream?"

Alana rolled open the big bottom freezer compartment for our inspection. It was filled with Lightweight Gourmet frozen TV dinners. And ice cubes. "Here, have another beer," she said, sliding a bottle across the table at Geneva. "It's supposed to be good for your hair."

Geneva was still working on her second bottle, *my bottle.* "She already has one," I protested, pushing the new one back to Alana.

"Leave that here!" Geneva commanded, glaring at me through watery eyes. "I'll drink it later." She finished my beer in big, noisy gulps and wiped her mouth on the back of her sleeve.

Alana's eyes followed the move, but she didn't complain. "I have an idea," she said slyly. "Why don't we go get ice cream at Yum Yum's?"

Geneva grinned at her. "You mean drive?"

Alana was as cool as an iceberg. "My mother's car is in the garage. She always leaves an extra key in the glove compartment. But we'd have to be back here by eleven."

Geneva picked up the unopened bottle of beer. "Let's take this along for the road."

"Shouldn't we change first? We don't want to call too much attention to ourselves," Deidre said. She had on Dr. Voegel-Whitcroft's tuxedo, complete with the ruffled shirt, bow tie, and cummerbund. Even if she were a man, she would have been pretty noticeable at Yum Yum's in that getup.

But Geneva said, "Why not? When we walk into Yum Yum's in these outfits, people's heads will spin like bar stools." To demonstrate, she laid her empty beer bottle on its side and spun it around.

She reminded me of a balloon cut loose from its cord, flying dizzyingly high. Once, after a day at the zoo, I'd let my balloon go, insisting on watching until it had completely disappeared from sight. The wait had irritated Mitchell, who'd asked, "You know what happens after they disappear?"

I was only four. "What?"

"They burst into smithereens," he'd answered smugly, and I'd cried all the way home.

"C'mon, Peace." Alana threw an arm around Geneva. "Anyone who wants to stay in her costume is welcome to come along. My mother has a big, fat Cadillac."

"Geneva, you just had two beers. Maybe you'd better wait a while . . . or take along a crash helmet." I wanted it to sound like a joke; instead I heard myself pleading.

"Relax, I'm steady as a rock." Geneva held out her hands and shook them exaggeratedly, which set the Barfettes off into torrents of laughter. Then, making sure I was still watching, she popped the cap off the third bottle.

"Seriously, driving now could be dangerous! Alcohol slows your reflexes," I insisted. I didn't care anymore if they all thought I was a wimp.

"Did you learn that playing Knowledge Bowl?" Geneva asked. She smiled at the others, who smirked back.

I found the hall closet and got my coat. Tears of frustration sprang to my eyes as I fumbled with the lock on the front door. Halfway down the street I heard Geneva call, "Hey, Andi, where are you going?"

"Home," I shouted over my shoulder.

"You're crazy! You must live ten miles from here."

"So?"

I kept walking, although a voice was shouting, "Andi, wait!" I didn't stop until I reached the end of the block. Then I turned around. Someone was running toward me.

It was Phoebe. "You can call your parents from my house. I live just around the corner," she offered between gasps.

I was still wearing Claudia's clothes when I got in the car with my father. If he noticed, he didn't let on until we pulled into the driveway. "Why don't you go in through the garage so you can make it to your room without running into your mother," he suggested.

21

s I pushed through Barf's broad oak door Monday morning, Phoebe caught my elbow. She must have been waiting for me. "Did you hear about the accident?"

A sickening feeling spread through my stomach, and I reached out to grab the wall for support. "What accident?"

"Don't worry, no one was hurt," she assured me, "but they sideswiped the inside of the garage as they backed out. That set off the automatic door opener, and the door closed on the trunk of the car. *Crunch!*"

I pictured Geneva, Alana, and the others gaping in shock as the garage door crushed the trunk of the "big, fat Cadillac." Right in the middle of the corridor, a snort of laughter burst through my nose. People in either direction stared like I was having a seizure or something.

"Caroline called to tell me," Phoebe said when I'd regained my composure. "She said Alana was really mad." The thought made her grin.

I started to giggle again, until I realized that Geneva could be in a lot of hot water, enough to wash a dozen

Cadillacs. "Did anyone get in trouble? I mean, Alana's parents didn't call the police, did they?" I asked.

"I'm not sure. Dr. Voegel-Whitcroft called all the parents, but I don't think he contacted the police." Phoebe looked around at the kids rushing by. "The first-period bell's going to ring in a minute. We'd better get going. See you later."

My thoughts were racing as I walked to class. If I hadn't abandoned Geneva at the party, maybe the accident wouldn't have happened. I knew how crazy she acted when she was upset. And what if Phoebe was wrong and Alana's father had called the police? Geneva was the driver *and* she'd been drinking. She could be in very serious trouble.

After I'd left Alana's party, I hadn't been sure I wanted to speak to Geneva ever again. But now I knew I had to call her the minute I got home this afternoon. If family members shouldn't give up on each other, neither should friends.

I walked into math, which was my first-period class, and took my seat behind Alana. As soon as she heard me, she spun around. "Your stupid friend Peace wrecked my mother's car. I'm grounded forever," she spat out as if it were my fault.

"So now I guess you'll have time to do your own homework." It was the best comeback I'd ever invented. I couldn't help thinking that in spite of all that had happened, it was a line that would make Geneva laugh. I'd have to remember to tell her.

• • •

176

Later, on the way home from school, I practiced what I wanted to say. *I'm sorry I walked out on you, but I was scared. . . . I'm not going to drive or drink or do anything else that's illegal anymore. . . . You really hurt my feelings.*

Ma was out, but I locked the door to my room anyway before I dialed Geneva's number. She picked up on the first ring. "Hello?"

"Hi, it's Andi." My voice came out like a whisper.

When she didn't say anything, I continued, "I heard about the accident. Did you get in a lot of trouble?"

"Sort of. Since my dad's paying for the damages to the car, Alana's father didn't call the police. But he insisted that my father 'alert the principal to my problem,' so everyone can 'keep an eye on my behavior.'" Her quotes had a cutting edge to them. "I'm supposed to see the school psychologist twice a week for a while, too. I guess they think I'm an alcoholic, or a car thief. Or maybe just a nut."

"At least you don't have to go to court," I said, groping for something positive to say. "How'd your dad take it?"

"When he found out I'd been driving around, he got pretty upset."

Terror made my stomach lurch. "He knows about the other times, too?"

She let out a long breath. "Yeah, I told him. Don't worry, I didn't mention your name."

"Wh-why'd you tell him?"

"I don't know. I just did."

Something in her tone kept me from saying the things I'd planned. But I had the dreamlike feeling that if I hung up now, she'd disappear. I wound the phone cord around my wrist like it was a lifeline. "So are you being grounded or what?"

"Kind of," she answered ambiguously.

"Will you be free by Christmas vacation? I was thinking maybe we could go visit Mitchell for my birthday." I giggled nervously. "By train, I mean. We could hang around the student union and pretend we're freshmen."

"I can't. I won't be here."

"You're going away for Christmas? Where?" I felt disappointed, but I told myself it might be a good thing. Maybe Mr. Peace was going to pay more attention to her now. A vacation might even help Geneva and Claudia get to know each other better. I pictured the three of them lounging on a beach somewhere, playing cards the way my family used to do before Mitchell went to college.

I could still hear Geneva breathing, but she didn't say anything for the longest time. Then she began talking really fast. "I was going to call you soon, Andi, really. You remember the video R.J. showed about the school in Israel, the one where American and Israeli kids study together?"

I didn't answer.

"I'll be starting there right after the vacation."

"Your father can't just send you away!" I shouted. "You're not a criminal! We'll call the—the child welfare bureau or something!"

"He's not sending me away," she murmured, so quietly I could scarcely hear her. "I asked to go."

I pressed my palm over my mouth and nose so she wouldn't hear me crying.

"Andi, I'm leaving, *but I'm not leaving you.* I'll write tons, and you can come visit me in the summer. We'll drive camels though the desert—you couldn't possibly need a license for that."

"No one in Israel rides around on camels except the Bedouins," I told her, laughing through my tears. "I can't believe you're going! You're my only real friend."

"We'll still be friends, Andi. *Forever.* You know how much I like that word."

"Yeah, but you'll make other friends in Israel," I murmured. "I've heard the kids mature pretty fast because of all the fighting over there. They'll probably be a lot like you." I thought back to the first day of Hebrew class, when Geneva seemed too sophisticated to ever even notice me. Suddenly I remembered something. "You know, I still have that bell bracelet you let me wear. I was going to give it back, but I never got around to it. I'll bring it over."

"No, keep it. That way, when I'm gone, I'll be able to think of you wearing it."

"Thanks. I'm really going to miss you!" I said fiercely.

"You'd better," she answered just as threateningly.

I was crying and smiling at the same time now. I knew she was, too.

22

$\mathcal{I}$ can't eat pizza or get in a car without thinking of Geneva. I miss her a lot, and I worry about her, too. She sounds happy in her letters, but I'd have to see her to really know.

Ma says living at a residential school will provide Geneva with the structure she needs, that it will give her a chance to "straighten out." Only what would a straightened-out Geneva be like? When I try to think about it, I get the willies. I picture her neat and complaisant with blank eyes, like some mannequin. A person without plans or schemes or secrets.

R.J. keeps trying to reassure me about it. He saw the American-Israeli School when he was in Israel three years ago—that's where he got the video he showed in class—and he says it's a terrific place. He thinks the buddy system they use to pair up each American student with an Israeli student will help Geneva break the ice right away. He also thinks Israel will be good for her "spirit of adventure." That part sounds right.

Mr. Peace and Claudia are planning to visit Geneva this summer. Actually, it's more than a visit; they've taken an apartment in Tel Aviv for June, July, and August so they can "work on building a new relationship" with Geneva. One day when I was thinking aloud, I said to Ma that maybe Geneva would even come back with them in September. She said not to expect miracles.

Except that two of them have happened already! The first is, Ma has actually agreed to let me visit Geneva. Mr. Peace and Claudia invited me to stay for all of August, although so far I only have permission to go for two weeks. I'm still working on my parents, though.

Mitchell is the other miracle. He came home over Christmas vacation, and it didn't go too badly. There was plenty of yelling and door slamming, but at least everyone's talking to each other. Here's what's supposed to happen: Mitch can stay in the apartment at school if he maintains a B average and comes home once every twelve weeks, including spending two weeks with us during the summer. Ma has to stay out of his room while he's home, as long as he cleans it before he leaves. And when he goes out at night, he doesn't have to say what he's doing unless he wants to, as long as he's in by two in the morning.

One night while he was still here, we were going through our old baseball card albums in his room. "Mitch, is this going to work?" I asked. "Are you really going to be coming home regularly now?"

"Who knows? Both Ma and I can be pretty stubborn. It's not really the rules we're fighting over. She just doesn't want me to grow up." He took off his baseball cap and pulled it down on my head.

I love that Mitch is honest with me, even though his answer made me sad. But I'm old enough to understand that not everything can be fixed right away. And some things maybe never. I still have my wish braid.

In her last letter to me, Geneva listed some of the things she wants us to do together when I get there: flirt with the soldiers stationed on the hilltops of Old Jaffa; eat falafel (she likes it better than pizza!) until we are sick of it; and swim in the Mediterranean Sea, which she swears is perfect turquoise. She signs her letters *Shalom, Geneva*.

Shalom means peace in Hebrew. Sometimes on Friday nights, if I am not at a meeting of *Barth Breezes*, the school literary magazine (yes, I finally took Ms. Taylor's advice), I attend services at Hillside. When we pray silently, I talk to God about Geneva. I ask that her heart be filled with peace.

Shalom, Geneva. Peace.